A EASTSIDE GANGSTA CHOSE ME TOO

NIDDA

A East Side Gangsta Chose Me Too

Copyright © 2017 by Nidda

Published by Mz. Lady P Presents

www.mzladypresents.com

ACKNOWLEDGMENTS

First, I would like to thank God for everything! Without him none of this would be possible. I would like to thank my parents for their love and support with everything. My aunt Lisa girl I owe you so much for never giving up on me and continuing to encourage me to keep going! & the rest of my family and friends that have been supportive I love y'all too! Mz Lady P for everything that you have done I will always be grateful! MLPP for being there to listen to my ideas and being supportive I appreciate y'all too!

To my readers I appreciate every one of you for giving me a chance! More is coming I don't plan on stopping anytime soon! S/O to Shay Shay, Janay, keyah, Mari and Rani! Y'all have all shown so much love! If I forgot anybody, please charge it to my head and not my heart! Anybody that has read a book by me, shared a post on social media, told someone about my books I truly appreciate it!!

KEEP UP WITH ME

FACEBOOK: NIDDA BIDDA

Facebook Reading Group: Nidda's Reading Spot
Instagram: _Nidda__
Twitter: _Nidda__
Thank you again! Don't forget to leave a Review.

KURUPT

As I sit here waiting for Enforcer to get back from dropping off the money in the tunnel, I'm losing my fucking mind, and Mina keeps calling me every five minutes. Now my momma is calling.

"Yea momma," I said as the call connected.

"I just called to check on you," Alice said.

I haven't been able to think about anything but Hope and the fact that this bitch Quita would take her and now want a fucking ransom. If anything is wrong with my baby, I'm going to kill that bitch's whole family. As I sit in the spot waiting for Enforcer to come back, this damn front door is opening too many fucking times.

"Everybody that doesn't need to be here get the fuck out! Naw, fuck that. Everybody get the fuck out!" I screamed.

Everybody made their way out the door. I know that my momma is concerned, but she's not helping either. I got her off the phone; I need to fucking think. E finally walked through the front door and Gotti came in behind him. I had sent Gotti to see what he could find out.

My phone started ringing, and it is a private number, so I know that it's the call that I'm waiting for. I answered the phone and whoever the fuck it is, Quita or her soon to be dead ass nigga, aren't saying anything. I'm screaming into the phone saying hello and then they just fucking hung up.

"What happened?" Gotti asked.

"Not shit, they not saying nothing," I said.

The phone started ringing again. I took a deep breath as I answered the phone and put it on speakerphone. I never imagined that I would be going through no shit like this. When Quita left, I did what the fuck I had to do for Hope, and this shit is really fucking with me. Right now, I have to stay strong and do what I have to do to make sure that Hope comes home.

"Bitch, where the fuck is my baby?" I spat.

"How are you doing, baby momma? I'm sorry I have been playing house with our baby with another bitch. That's how the fuck you should be talking to me," Quita said, laughing.

"Quita, you got the money, so just tell me where my baby is at," I said, trying not to go off while she has my baby.

"Enforcer, I love Envii's new Lexus. It's really cute. So, get me one K, and then I guess you can have your daughter back. I'll have to see maybe or maybe not," Quita said.

I know Quita, I know how scandalous she is, and I know the type of shit that she used to do. For her to be doing this shit and using my baby to get money and shit just shows how trifling she is. I handed E the phone and walked out the house to get some air before I go off and that bitch does some more fucked up shit.

I grabbed my burner out the armrest of my car and called Bad News. I need to get some more people in the streets to see what the fuck is going on, and Bad News can get everybody rounded up. I need people watching her momma, auntie and everybody else that this bitch might be in contact with so that I can find my fucking baby. Who knows how long she plans on playing this game. I know that it is a nigga that got her making these types of demands. Quita thinks fifty dollars is some money, so she has no idea what to do with hundred thousand. E and Gotti made their way outside, and I jumped out the car to see what is going on now.

"I called Dan at the dealership. I'm on my way up there now," E said, handing me my phone back.

"Alright, call me if y'all hear anything," I said as I made my way to my car. I have to get out here too.

Bad News has sent word to get everybody that is affiliated to hit the streets. I'm not going to sleep until I have Hope. When I get my hands on that bitch, I'm going to kill that bitch slow. I made my way over to where Quita's mom used to live. As I ride, I can't help but think what the fuck that bitch could be doing to my baby. She cut her fucking ponytail off. All the possibilities of what it could be going on are making me even fucking madder.

Quita's playing games with me. Now, her wanting a car doesn't surprise me. Her laughing about this shit, and her already being able to imagine where my head is at is going to make her keep playing this game as long as she can. I pulled up on Peoria to the house that Cassie used to live in, and it's white people going inside. I knew as I drove over here there is a chance that she wouldn't live here anymore.

I have to go and check on Mina and talk to Brionna so that I can see if she can do something for me. I know that Mina is good with Brionna. Looking in my rearview mirror at Hope's car seat is fucking me up. People do all types of crazy shit to kids. If somebody does something to me, I can handle it and defend myself my baby can't. As I pulled up at Bad News' place, my phone is ringing, and it's Krack. I don't have time to talk to him right now, so I sent him to the voicemail.

Mina opened the door and fell into my arms still crying. I got her into the house, and she is asking questions that I don't have the answers to. I can't tell Mina that. Mina is used to me being the one that handles everything. In her eyes, I can solve everything and make everything okay. Not being able to fix this is making me sick to my stomach. I finally got Mina to calm down and go lay down.

"Bri, I need to you to look up some people for me," I said.

"Alright, let me go and get my laptop," Brionna said and disappeared.

Bri can do all types of shit. She's a professional at falsifying some shit. I got three ID's that ain't in my name. I know that Bri can find up to date info on all of Quita's family and hopefully Quita too. In minutes, Bri started to rattle off addresses for everybody I asked for. I should have done this shit from the beginning.

"Cassie Jones is a resident at a nursing home," Brionna said.

As soon as visiting hours start I'll be there waiting for Quita. If she is here in Colorado, I know that she'll be to see her momma bright and early. I'm getting impatient waiting for E to call me and let me know what is happening with the damn car. We buy cars all the time, drive off, come back, and do the paperwork later, so I don't see what the fuck is taking so long.

"You know some nigga named O?" I asked.

Brionna knows a lot of muthafuckas in her business, and if she knows this nigga, then I think that he might be able to lead me to Quita. First, he starts popping up on the block and then Quita showing up. That can't be any fucking coincidence. I got everybody on the lookout for that nigga. He has been on the block asking about me, so he shouldn't be that hard to find. Brionna doesn't who the nigga is, but she grabbed her phone to call some people to see what she can find out. Shit, I don't know anything about the nigga, so I can't even give a good fucking description of who he is.

My phone started ringing, and it's Bad News. He confirmed they had O. I let Brionna know and made my way to talk to Mina before I leave. She's asleep, so I just left her alone. I have to get to this bitch nigga and see where the fuck Quita is. I made my way out to my car and headed to the spot where they got this nigga at.

I jumped out. Dirt and Gotti were standing by the door, and I can hear Envii from way out here. *What the fuck is she doing here?* I thought her and E weren't even speaking to each other. I'm not in the mood to deal with her loud ass. When I walked into the spot, Envii surprisingly shut the fuck up. This nigga looks untouched like they just snatched him and brought him here and that is a problem for me.

"Lower him," I said as I walked to the middle of the floor where he is hanging.

We haven't had to use this spot in a long time. I kept it just for emergencies like this one. They got this nigga hanging upside down in chains with his arms and legs both spread in a different direction. I looked at Envii because I know she's the one that decided this was a good way to restrain him.

"I know I did a good muthafucking job. I'll give you some kidnapping tips before we leave," Envii said.

I shook my head and turned back around to this nigga. O is knocked out, and I know Envii's dumb ass didn't think of him passing the fuck out from the blood rushing to his fucking head. She should have stayed her ass in school. I took out my lighter and started to burn his face with it, and he woke right up. As big as his eyes got he knows exactly who the fuck I am.

"So, I hear you been looking for me. What's up?" I said.

He didn't say anything just started to choke uncontrollably looking around. O is lying flat on his back still in chains and on the concrete. I lost all the patience I had dealing with Quita earlier. That bitch got the car, and I still don't have my daughter.

"Get him something to drink," I said, and Dirt went to get it.

"This that bitch now," E said, walking out the warehouse.

Dirt came back handed me the can filled with gasoline. It's filled to the top and started to come out the funnel. I don't have all night, and this nigga is about to start talking one way or another. I pushed my Glock into his mouth, knocking out a few teeth in the process, opened up his mouth, and proceeded to pour the gas down his throat. Enforcer came back into the room.

"This bitch is making more requests, K," E said.

I nodded my head, looked back at O, and watched him squirm and move like he was going to be able to bust out of these chains. Some muthafuckas are just dumb and even though this is fucking extreme, and I don't know why the fuck Envii did this shit, I do know that fucking with her ass he ain't getting out of this shit.

"Where is my daughter?" I asked.

"I don't know. After she got the money, she left, and I haven't seen her since," O struggled to say.

I know her broke ass did. She didn't want to have to split the money with his ass or give him none of it. He ran down the motel that they were staying at, and Envii left out to go and look for her, but I know that bitch ain't staying there with the money that she's got in her hands. He gave me the address to all the places that Bri had already given me.

I started to pour the gas all over O, and Dirt handed me a piece a paper. I lit it and threw it on him. I've got to get to the nursing home to see Momma Cassie.

GOTTI

"What do you want now, Giordan?"

"Can you come by?" Giordan asked.

"You know I'm not. Gionni is at my house, so what the fuck would I need to come to your house for?"

Giordan is Gionni's mother and nothing else. Gionni is with me majority of the time. I haven't fucked with Giordan in years, and the only reason why I talk to her now is because of Gionni. Giordan started to say something, and I just hung up on her. Gionni is thirteen, and I haven't fucked with Giordan since she was pregnant. You only get one time to play me, and after that, yo muthafuckin' ass will not get another chance. The only reason why she's still alive is because of Gionni.

As I pulled up at home, I see Envii's car. Goddess is going to outpatient treatment trying to save face for her coworkers and these bougie muthafuckas neighbors. It's a damn shame that I don't even want to go in my own house because of Envii's loud ass. I can hear her loud ass from out here. I made my way in the house. Goddess was coming down the stairs as I walked in the house.

"Hi, baby! How was your day?" Goddess asked.

"It was alright, you good?"

I love my wife, and I don't know what the fuck I would do without her. She understands me and is my peace from the streets. Goddess is beautiful with smooth caramel skin, big pretty brown eyes, and long straight black hair that is all hers. My wife is tall and thick in all the right places. Goddess is damn near perfect. She's smart, understanding, and loyal.

We have good days and bad days just like everybody else, but the good outweighs the bad. I know why Goddess is with me, and I know why I choose to be with her. At the time, we both needed each other for various reasons. I still feel the same way about her that I did when we first got together.

"Your mom called," Goddess said.

"Alright, I'll call her."

As we made our way through the house, my head started to pound. Envii is on the phone screaming at the top of her lungs. It is only so much of her ass that I can take. I don't see how the fuck Enforcer deals with that shit.

"Bitch, just do yo muthafucking job! Did I hire you to be a muthafucking *Cheaters* investigator? No bitch, I didn't! Unless you would like to sit in the dark and not make it to Christmas, I suggest you remember that!" Envii screamed into the phone and threw the phone across the room.

"If you want to break shit, I suggest you take yo ass home," I said as Goddess was attempting to step in between Envii and me.

"Move, Goddess!" I spat.

"Genesis, let me deal with Envii," Goddess pleaded.

"Fuck you! This is my sister's house too!" Envii spat.

"Envii, shut up, or you can leave," Goddess said.

The only thing that stopped me from shooting Envii was Goddess and my nigga E. I don't allow anybody to talk to me crazy. If the bitch at Conoco gets crazy, it will be some niggas waiting for her to finish her shift. Envii is so disrespectful, and she thinks she can talk to anybody any kind of way. I understand from being with Goddess that she and Envii have been through a lot. They mom wasn't shit, and neither were their dads. Envii uses that shit as an excuse to act the way she does. The bitch needs to go to therapy. My phone started vibrating. I looked at it it's my dumb ass cousin, Memphis.

"Dad, I don't have to go to my mom's, do I?" Gionni asked as she ran into the living room.

"No, you don't."

She handed me her phone with messages from Giordan saying she had to come home. I deleted all the messages and handed her back her phone. This is the type of shit that makes me want to fuck Giordan up.

"Is your homework done?"

"Yea."

Giordan is going to make me hurt her. Just when I thought I could come home and relax, that's out the fucking question. I got up and grabbed my jacket. Goddess met me at the door.

"Envii's leaving and Janice is on her way over," Goddess said.

"Good, I'll be right back. I gotta go handle something."

"Don't do anything to Giordan, Genesis."

I kissed Goddess and made my way out the door. Goddess and I don't discuss my business. She knows what I do, and she knew what it was before we went on our first date, but she wants no parts in that part of my life. Janice is Goddess' sponsor. So hopefully, she is gone by the time I get back. She also knows the situation with Giordan. Giordan didn't give a fuck about me again until I got with Goddess. I made my way to Giordan's to make sure this bitch understands a few things.

I'm so damn mad as I got out of my truck that I left the door opened and didn't give a fuck. If any of these muthafuckas think about touching my truck, they know what time it is. Giordan lives in the hood because she wants to pocket every dime she gets from me or anybody else. I pushed open Giordan's door, and it slammed into the wall. The picture that hung of her dead Aunt Mable shattered and hit the floor. I don't give a fuck. I made my way up the stairs to find her.

"Giordan!" I screamed.

"Don't come in my house breaking shit. Take yo ass back to that bit..." Giordan attempted to say before I snatched her off her bed by her neck.

"Bitch, don't ever in yo life try to use my daughter to get to me. If you ever refer to my wife as anything other than her name bitch, you'll go missing."

Giordan started gasping for air, but I didn't give a fuck. Giordan's damn near white skin is turning red. To a nigga in the streets, you would look at Giordan and say she bad, but even though she is pretty on the outside, she's an ugly muthafucka on the inside. The bitch wanted me to come over, so I'm here. As I looked at Giordan with her eyes bulging, I thought about Gionni and dropped her to the floor.

"Gionni won't be back here unless she decides she wants to see you. Don't call her, don't text her, and if you show up at her school, I will kill yo momma faster than she's already dying."

I made my way out the house. Giordan was still gasping for air. It didn't matter to me. I needed to get to Memphis' dumb ass. As I made my way to Memphis, Kurupt's number flashed across the dashboard. With all the shit that is going on right now, I can only imagine what the fuck he is about to say.

"What's up, K? I said as the call connected.

"I'm waiting for E to get back and this fucking phone to ring. I need you to do something for me," K said.

"Say no more. As soon as I handle this other shit real fast, I'm on my way," I said and disconnected the call.

I called this bitch ass nigga Memphis back, and he didn't answer. I called his ass again, and he still didn't answer. I have been waiting for this nigga to do his fucking job for days now. Family or not, this nigga is getting too damn comfortable, and today is the day his ass is going on notice.

"Muthafucka, where you at so that we can get this shit over wit?" I spat as the call connected.

"I'm in the middle of taking care of some—" Memphis attempted to say.

"I don't give a fuck if you were painting yo nails, bitch! Where the fuck is you at?" I screamed into the phone.

"I'm at my baby momma's," Memphis said, breathing hard in my damn ear.

Memphis has one job to transport guns and nothing else. The only reason I have him doing that is because he's getting them from his brother. I'll figure something else out because this isn't working.

"I was just trying to tell you that I'm ready."

"Nigga, what you ready for? You got one job, and if that ain't working for you, I suggest you figure something else out."

All these calls and texts in between are fucking unnecessary. I don't have time to sit on the phone with no damn body. Memphis had been blowing up my phone trying to meet up, but then he can only do it at a specific time. This nigga is slow, and I'm convinced that he should be getting a fucking check.

"I know, but I can do more..."

"Look, muthafucka. After this next time coming up. I'm done with yo ass. Do not fucking leave that house until I get there or you're dead."

I don't have patience, and clearly, he thinks because we're cousins he gets some special pass, but he doesn't. I'm not giving my momma pass, or nobody else's momma a pass. I don't know why muthafuckas insist on playing with me today. Momma flashed across the dashboard.

"Yes, momma," I said.

"Genesis, come by so that we can to talk," my mother Nancy said.

"Alright I'm on my way," I said and disconnected the call.

I know why she is calling me, and it's not because she fucking wants to talk. We talk enough. I made my way over to my momma's so that I can get this shit over with and get to Memphis. I pulled up and jumped out. I wish she would leave this house, but she refuses to. I see my sister Modesty's car in the driveway, and she is supposed to be at school. The school I'm paying all this fucking money for her to go to for her black ass not to be there. I let myself in, and Modesty damn near jumped off the couch when she saw me.

"Why the fuck is you not at school?" I asked.

"I needed a break," Modesty said, shrugging her shoulders.

"I'm going to break yo fucking face if you don't get the fuck out of here and go to school," I said, walking up on Modesty.

Modesty is eighteen, and she lives with Goddess and me. The only time she comes over here is when she on some good bullshit because she knows that she can get away with that shit over here. It's not about the money, but I want Modesty to something with her life and get the fuck out of here. She's not going to do that from over here sitting on the couch with momma. Modesty hugged and kissed my mom and made her way to the door.

"Either you go to school, or I'm taking my fucking car, and yo ass will be on the bus!" I screamed before the front door closed behind Modesty.

I handed my momma what the fuck she wanted and the reason why she was calling me. You can say the fuck you want to say about me, but if she doesn't get it from me, then she's going to get it from the nigga around the corner! It's not about the money. I can't buy toilet paper to fill the bathrooms in my house for a month with the money I get from my mom. I don't want my mom out on here getting shit from any of these niggas out here. My mom has been on drugs for years ever since my dad left her. I can't make her get help. She doesn't want help, and I accepted that a long time ago.

Before then we had a damn near perfect family. My mother was teaching school, and my father was a preacher. I met Enforcer at church; our dads were good friends. One night my mom picked up the phone and heard my dad on the phone with some deacon from the church talking about how he wanted to suck his dick. My mom confronted him while he was on the phone, and they got into an argument. He left, and I haven't seen him since that night.

Ever since that night, my mom has never been the same. We never talked about it; we just acted like it never happened. My mom hasn't stepped foot in a church since that happened and neither have I. That's why when Goddess and I got married, I wouldn't get married in a church. Modesty was so young that I don't even think that she would remember it happened.

"How is Goddess doing?" my mother asked.

"She's alright. I have to go. We are still looking for Hope," I said as I kissed my mom on the cheek, picked up my money off the coffee table, and made my way out the door.

KAI MORAE

I 'm trying to focus and keep my eyes open. This is the worst headache that I ever had in my life. I'm looking around the room trying to weigh my options on what the fuck I am going to do to get out of here. I can hear Memphis in the other room talking, but I don't hear Deontae.

I don't have any time to waste and laying on this floor crying and thinking about and blaming myself for all the fucked-up decisions that I made isn't going to get me anywhere. I'm struggling to get off the floor and not lose my balance. I started to bang on the bedroom door while praying that Deontae isn't here right now. I'm not sure what time it is, but it's now dark outside.

I can hear somebody putting a key in the door, so I stopped knocking. I backed up from the door so whoever it is can get in. Luckily, it is Memphis, and he's dumber that Deontae, so I can play his ass easier.

"You want some water?" Memphis said, handing me a bottle of water.

"Thank you," I said, taking the water and taking it to the head.

Memphis phone started ringing. Whoever it is mad as fuck and calling him all types of punk bitches. I know that if Deontae were here, he would have been in here getting Memphis the fuck out of my face. So, he must be gone somewhere.

"Can you hand me my purse so that I can get a Tylenol out of it?" I said.

Memphis jumped and went to get my bag. I finished off the bottle of water, and I'm still thirsty. Memphis came back still on the phone and handed me my bag. I found what the fuck I needed, and it's not a damn Tylenol. I pulled out Sean's gun and put it to Memphis' head. His eyes got as big as golf balls, and he dropped his phone to the ground. When the phone smacked the ground, a nigga said that he was outside. I shot Memphis in his head, and he slapped the tiled floor, causing a loud thump to echo throughout the room.

I've been around guns most of my life, but actually pulling a trigger was something that I never thought that I would have to do. I can't stop looking at Memphis' lifeless body lying in front of me. His eyes are wide open, and even though I know he is dead and isn't breathing, it's like he is looking straight at me.

"Kai," I heard a man's voice say.

I looked up pointing the gun in the man's direction, and it's Gotti. He tried to grab the gun out of my hand, but I still have a tight grip on it. Gotti was able to snatch the gun from my hand. I don't know why he is here, but I have never been so damn happy to see him in my life.

"Kai, come on. You got to get out of here. Go to my truck, and I'll be right out," Gotti said putting, his truck keys in my hand.

I snapped out of the daze I was in and snatched up my purse from the ground and got the fuck out of the house. With each step I take, it feels like pins and needles are sticking me. My entire body is in pain, but right now, none of that shit matters. Even though Gotti and I never had a close relationship, the way that K always talked about him I know that he is a real one and will handle everything.

"Pop the trunk!" Gotti hollered from outside the truck.

I popped the trunk, and Gotti put two oversized duffle bags in the trunk and went back and did a light jog back to the house. I went through my purse looking for a Tylenol to take until I can get to something stronger. Gotti came back to the trunk with two more duffle bags slammed the trunk and got in.

As we drove, I don't know what the fuck to say to Gotti. How do I explain what happened back there when I know he knows how things ended between Kamal and me all because of what the fuck I chose to do. I'm ashamed that I put myself in a position for that shit to happen to me.

"Thank you, Gotti," I finally said.

"You good," Gotti said and kept bobbing his head to the Jeezy that is coming out of his speakers.

Now that I am out of there, I have to figure out what the fuck I am going to do. Deontae had emptied out my bank account, and I'm sure he found my stash at the house and took that too. With him still being alive, I can't go back to my apartment. I'm damn sure not going back to my Aunt Lisa's. We pulled up to Gotti and Goddess' home. I looked at the time before I got out the truck, and it's damn near three in the morning.

"You can stay here for the night," Gotti said as he led the way into their place.

Their house is beautiful. It reminds me a lot of K's place. I've only been over here once, and it looks like they have made a lot of changes since then. I feel like a fucking bum, and I know that I look like one too. The fact that I know that Gotti is going to tell Kamal that he saw me and my current position is what embarrasses me the most. Goddess is running down the left side of their double staircase as I walked in the house.

Gotti disappeared, and Goddess was being her normal self. She is willing to help anybody and by doing all that she can. She led the way to one of their nine bedrooms. She keeps offering me food and something to drink. Goddess is a truly good person and has a heart made of gold with no malice or ill intentions. By the concern in her face, as she looked over my body, the scars, bruises, and the overall condition that I am in, I know that she has questions, but she hasn't asked them.

"Goddess, I'm fine. I appreciate you and Gotti letting me stay here," I said.

"You already know that I will help you any way that I can, and Gotti must think you're okay otherwise he would have left you where he found you at," Goddess said, laughing.

Goddess has clothes and pajamas with the tags laid out on the bed. I'm guessing that they must be Modesty's because they damn sure ain't Goddess' size. Goddess showed me where everything that I would need is to be able to get myself together and somebody started knocking on the door. I turned to see who it was, and it's Gotti.

"Here this should help with some of the pain. If you don't feel better in the morning Goddess will call her people to come see about you," Gotti said, handing me two pills and leaving back out the room.

"I'm going to call my friend Dr. Maci. I think you need someone to check you out just in case," Goddess said.

All I want to do is get in the hot steaming shower and go to sleep. I know that it is going to hurt like hell, but right now that is all I want. I will deal with everything else when I wake up. I need to call Katrina back. She has called me so many damn times, but I'll do that in the morning because that is probably where I'm going to be living.

"If you need anything, we are at the very end of the hallway," Goddess said.

"I'll be fine. You have done more than enough," I said.

I don't know what all Gotti has told Goddess about what happened earlier. I also don't know what she knows about K and me. I am going to get some rest and come up with a plan. Gotti is always very short with everybody. I have never heard him say too much, so he is hard to read. If he didn't really want me here, I would never know unless he said it. I know that I can't live here, so I have to do what the fuck I know how to do and make a way out of no way.

* * *

As I opened my eyes, it's still dark outside. I feel like I have been sleeping forever. I grabbed my phone off the nightstand, and I have twenty missed calls. It's nine o'clock at night. I have to get up and get out of here. I slipped off the clothes that Goddess gave me and called Katrina. Her ass is going to have to come and get me.

"Bitch, where have you been?" Katrina screamed in the phone.

"I'll tell you in a minute. I need you to come and get me," I said as Goddess knocked on the door of the bedroom.

"You're up, how are you feeling?" Goddess asked.

I told Katrina that I would text her the address and got off the phone with her. If staying at her house dealing with her and her nigga for the week doesn't make me get my shit together fast, then nothing will.

"I'm feeling better. I'm going to go on head and go," I said, looking through my purse.

"You do not have to go, Kai. You can stay here as long as you need to," Goddess said.

"Kai, get yo shit and come on," I heard a man say.

I looked up at the door, and it's Kamal. The look in his eyes is one that I have never seen before. Goddess knows something because she snatched my charger out the wall and handed me some shoes. Kamal left from the doorway, and I can hear him and Gotti talking. Goddess told me to call her and was helping me off the bed like I'm crippled. I can't say that I am not happy to see K, but knowing that Deontae is still out here, I don't want to bring any of that to him.

Goddess and I made our way out of the room. K and Gotti are standing at the bottom of the staircase. The hate that is in K's eyes is making me uncomfortable and uneasy. I know that I deserve it all for how I played the situation, and the situation that I am in now, all I can hope is that he will hear me out.

As Goddess walked me out to K's truck, he opened the door and got in the driver side slamming the door making the windows shake. I got in the truck and Tupac "When We Ride on Our Enemies" started to blast through the speakers as K started up the truck and sped off. K hasn't looked at me or said one word. Every time his phone rings he looks at it and keeps ignoring the calls. I can't say anything about him being cold and not being the loving man that he was when I first met him. As he turned the corner, I grabbed the armrest that his arm was resting on, and he snatched his arm away. Tears started to form in my eyes, and before I knew it, they are falling down my face faster than I can wipe them.

K pulled up to a home that is a few blocks away from Gotti's. He slammed the car in park, grabbed his phone, and called somebody saying, "Hold 'em," and hung up.

K turned down the music that is making my headache worse than it already is. I checked my phone and Katrina is calling me. I sent her to voicemail. I'll call her back in a minute.

"Kamal, I'm sorr—" I attempted to say before he threw up his hand, which caused me to jump.

"You think I'm gone hit you? You have been fucking with that bitch nigga too long. I don't want to hear that shit so save it," Kamal said, reaching over me and opening the glove compartment, taking out an envelope.

A black Audi pulled up into the circular driveway facing us. The nigga in the car nodded his head. I want to apologize for everything that I have done. I know I was wrong, and I knew it shortly after I did it. It didn't take for me to go through that shit last night to know that Deontae wasn't shit. He showed me his true colors a long time ago.

"Stay here. Go to work, school and come back here. You can drive the Lexus truck in the garage. If you need anything Ace or Big Face will make sure that you get it," K said, putting the envelope in my lap.

A nigga opened the truck door, and I looked at Kamal as he switched the truck into drive and wouldn't look at me still. I got out the truck and made my way into the house. I looked back hoping that Kamal was coming in, but he sped out of the driveway, causing me to cry harder than I was. I looked out the window, and the nigga that pulled up in the Audi is still sitting out there. I pulled out my phone, and Gina has called me three times. I dialed 611 to change my phone number right now.

I hear a phone ringing, so I made my way through the house to find it. I'm still waiting for slow ass T-Mobile to answer the fucking phone. This house is amazing, but being in this big ass house alone is making me feel more alone than I already am. The phone stopped ringing as I came upon a big ass living room with fish tanks covering one of the long ass walls. The phone started ringing again, and I see it across the room on an end table. I struggle to get over to it since I am still fucked up. I picked up the phone, and nobody said anything.

"When I call this phone you need to answer," K said.

"Okay."

"Nobody needs to know where the fuck you at, but me," K said and disconnected the call.

An operator at T-Mobile finally came on the line, and I told her to change my number. She put me on hold. I don't give a fuck today how long I need to hold on this number is getting changed today. Katrina is blowing up my phone, but she is going to have to wait. I made my way upstairs and walked room to room taking all of this in. Every room is fully furnished with bedroom suites and TVs on the walls. I made it all the way down the hall to the last room and opened the door. This has to be the master bedroom because it is the biggest room.

It is a California king bed with a cushioned headboard. Curtains hanging from the ceiling on the sides of the bed are pulled back to the wall. I made my way to the closet, and it is filled with clothes. They are color coordinated in each section of the closet. The shoe racks are filled with tennis shoes and heels of every kind that you could want. I spotted a chaise chair that matches the décor and laid down on it. The fucking lady at T-Mobile finally did whatever she needed to do and got my number changed.

As I lay here, I can't help, but to think about what I am going to do. Yes, K has put this together for me, but I need to be able to handle shit on my own. I can't stay here forever. He won't even look at me and doesn't want to hear shit that I have to say. I picked up my phone. I need to call Katrina back. Her ass didn't answer, so I texted her, and she texted back saying she is on the phone with Enforcer. I thought I was fucking dumb. Bitches ain't shooting up my house for no nigga.

The doorbell is ringing, so I got up to see who it is. It's probably the nigga that K has watching me. I made my way downstairs, and it's Goddess, so I opened the door. She is always so happy and in good spirits. I'm just happy that somebody is here if only for a little while. "I brought some food over for you, so won't have to worry about cooking tonight," Goddess said as she led the way through the house.

"Thanks, but you didn't have to do that."

I know that. Everybody isn't out to get you, and there are some good people left in the world, but they are far and few in between in my life. As I jumped up on a barstool in the kitchen, the doorbell rang again, and Goddess made her way out to go and get it. I'm glad she bought some food because I'm fucking starving.

"Why the fuck did he move her to this house instead of just of just moving her to the house, and why is Ace's bitch ass sitting outside?" Envii asked loud as hell. Goddess is all the way down the hall, but I can still hear her.

"Envii, shut up damn. I don't know," Goddess said.

"Damn," Envii said as she walked into the room taking in how fucked up I am.

Goddess hit Envii and Envii made her way around sit next to me. Goddess is one thing, but Envii is a whole another breed of female, so hearing her opinion about the shit I've done I know is going to be way different than what Goddess is going to have to say. Goddess is putting a salad together, and it's awkward and too damn quiet for me.

"I'm not like Goddess. I'm not about to come over here cook for you. Bitch, I don't cook for myself. What the fuck happened and start from the beginning. Why the fuck did you leave K?" Envii said, breaking the awkward silence.

Goddess stopped what she was doing to turn around and face me. I started from the beginning telling them about Quan. Envii cut me right the fuck off, but Goddess shut her up, so I got back to telling them everything. The way Envii is looking at me, I don't know if she wants to fight or to just cut my ass off again. Goddess is just shaking her head and looking at me with so much sympathy. I told them everything that happened at the house with Memphis and shit that was it. They know what happened with K, shit I'm here.

"I'm just going to be honest with you. You're fucking dumb," Envii said, taking a drink of juice.

"I'll take that. I fucked up," I said.

"So, what the fuck did K say to you?" Envii asked.

"Nothing," I said.

"Both of y'all are dumb and y'all belong together. I wouldn't have a bitch in my house and not address our fucking issues. I would have called you all types of stupid, dumb bitches, beat yo ass, and then depending on how bad I fucked you up maybe I'd let you stay," Envii said and then walked out of the room to take a call.

"Please excuse my sister. She doesn't know how to talk to people. K has a lot going on with Hope missing. Right now, nothing matters until Hope gets home," Goddess said as she went back to getting the food ready.

"Missing? What is going on?" I asked.

Goddess started to tell me everything that is going on. Hope has been missing for two days. They paid the first ransom, and now they have a second one, and Hope still is not home. I feel even worse than I already felt. I'm sitting here feeling sorry for myself for some shit that I got myself in, and Hope is fucking missing. I know how much K loves and cares about Hope, so I can't even imagine what he is going through.

"So, I have to go run and get this bitch out of the closet," Envii said as she came back into the kitchen.

"Out of a closet?" Goddess asked.

"Yes, bitch I know that device is working in your ear. Out of a closet. She should have been doing her fucking job, and she wouldn't have had to be in the damn closet," Envii said.

I have seen Envii in action, and I know after what she did at Katrina's, putting a bitch in a closet is nothing compared to what the fuck else she will do. Goddess and Envii are like oil and water. All they do is argue whenever I have ever been around them. I can't believe they even talk to each other.

"Come ride with me so that we can finish talking," Envii said.

"I can't," I said.

"You physically can't walk. I thought that you just got beat up a little bit," Envii said, moving her hands.

"No, K doesn't want me to leave the house," I said.

"So, he brought you here to be a house slave. Goddess while I'm gone tell this bitch when slavery ended," Envii said and made her way out the house.

My phone started going off alerting me that I have a message on messenger. I looked, and it's a message from my cousin Reign saying that my cousin Dink got shot.

KURUPT

"**M**r. Jones, can we get you anything?" Nurse Pam asked, for the hundredth fucking time.

"No, ma'am, I'm fine."

I have been sitting at Grace and Joy's nursing home for going on two days looking at this bitch's mom. She hasn't been here, but I have feeling that as soon as I leave that is when the bitch is going to come. It's a small facility, and the parking lot is really fucking small, so I had Dirt come pick up my car.

"Your sister is on her way up now, and I didn't tell her that you were here so that you can surprise her," Pam said.

"Thanks."

I sent Bad News and Brionna text in a group message letting them know I was ready. I've been telling these people that Quita is my sister and Cassie is my mom since I been up here. I'm visiting from out of town, and I want to surprise Quita is what I keep telling them, and they fucking believed it.

"Shut the fuck up! You'll see yo dad when I say you can see yo dad and not moment before! Do you fucking hear me?" I heard Quita scream from down the hall.

Hearing Hope scream at the top her lungs is making me fucking mad. Knowing that I can't start shooting in this fucking building is the only thing saving Quita from getting got right now. I can hear Pam talking to Quita in the hallway and giving her an update on Cassie's status. As soon as Quita walked into the room and seen my face, all the color drained from her brown skin.

"Aren't you so excited to see your brother?" Pam asked.

"How about you get out they damn business and leave them alone," Brionna said from behind them.

"Dad!" Hope screamed, running in my direction.

I'm not worried about Quita trying to do anything, Brionna has a mag digging the barrel in her back. As tears start to fall from Quita's eyes, all I can do is think about all the tears that my baby shed over the past four days. Hope is squeezing the fuck out my neck.

Brionna pushed Quita into the room, and I got out of the chair that I'm sitting in and stood with Hope still in my arms. Quita has light brown skin, and she's short and chubby now. She has a short curly wig on, Brionna wasn't feeling it, so she snatched it off and made Hope laugh. Seeing my baby smile made my day, and I smiled too. Something I haven't been able to do since she's been gone.

Brionna took the bag Quita is carrying off her arm, and I unzipped it. The money she isn't wearing on her back and in jewelry is still all in the bag. She still is fucking dumb as a box of fucking rocks. All I can do is shake my head.

"Where is Mina? Can we call Kai dad?" Hope asked.

"We're going to see Mina right now," I said and kissed Hope on the check.

Cassie is highly sedated from a surgery she had two days ago. She hasn't opened her eyes in the two days I've been here. Brionna has on scrubs matching all the nurses and CNA's here. I'm not worried about her being up here while I'm gone. Cassie's eyes popped open, and tears started to form in her eyes while looking at Hope and me.

"Tell yo momma goodbye. You'll be going see yo nigga O very shortly," I said, making my way out the door.

"Bye Bri!" Hope screamed as we walked down the hallway.

* * *

"MINA, MINA, WAKE UP!" Hope screamed, jumping on Mina.

"Leave me alone and go get K, Hope. I'm tired!" Mina said, swatting at Hope.

"You better get the fuck up, swatting at my baby," I said, hitting Mina with a pillow.

Mina finally got her ass up and grabbed Hope and tears started falling from her eyes. I can't help but tear up because I know how worried Mina has been about Hope. Before Hope was born, it was just Mina and me, but since Hope has been here, it has been us three. I handle business, but I am at home as much as I can be. I know that it's important that I am always there for them. Alice has been back in the picture here lately, but other than that we are all that we have.

"Come on. We got to go to see Goddess," I said as Mina continued to hug Hope.

I stepped out the room to holla at Ace. If he's over here, then Big Face must be watching Kai. Bad News came in the house, and I gave him the word to get on that other thing immediately. It had to go on the backburner until I had Hope back.

"K, Krack called," Mina said as she and Hope made it into the foyer.

"Alright, I'll call him," I said as we made our way out the house.

I don't know what talking to Krack is going to do at this point. We have been through this shit before, and I don't have shit to say. If Mina wants to have a relationship with him, then that is her decision. Right now, I have other shit to worry about.

As we rode down the street, Hope was showing Mina all the stuff she just got, and I can feel Mina's attitude coming into the front seat. Mina has never asked me for something, and she didn't get it, except this apartment that she been asking for.

"Where is my stuff at?" Mina asked.

I threw the Neiman Marcus bags in her face as I pulled into Gotti's driveway. She gets on my damn nerves. I got Hope out the truck, and we made our way into the house. I see Dr. Maci's car out here, so I'm starting to feel uneasy thinking about what the fuck she might tell me.

I would hope that Quita wouldn't have fucked with my baby, but I don't know who the fuck she had her around. She could have had her around any of her scandalous ass family. Fucked up uncles that everybody now knows done fucked with kids.

We have used Maci for some time now. She and Goddess have been friends for a long time. I can't take Hope to her regular doctor. How the fuck I'm going to explain any of this shit to them, so that is why we keep Maci on retainer. We made our way into the room that Maci set up to check Hope. I took Hope home when I first got her back and gave her bath, and she seemed to be okay, but I'm not a doctor.

Watching Maci check Hope is making me uncomfortable and she ain't saying nothing. Goddess keeps going back and forth between Ahmina and me, rubbing our backs and telling us that it will everything is going to be okay. I know that Goddess is just trying to help and soothe us, but she is getting on my damn nerves.

"Everything looks fine. There are not any tears or anything. There hasn't been any penetration or coercion done to Hope, Kamal," Maci said.

I am so relieved that was something that has been on my mind and knowing that none of that happened has me fucking relieved. I see every day on the news people doing shit to their kids or the fucking babysitter. That shit would fuck me up, and I don't know how the fuck I would deal with that. I got Hope dressed and handed Maci an envelope for leaving work to come and check Hope out.

"I was going to come over and bring you guys some food," Goddess said still rubbing Mina's back.

"We are good Goddess, I know how to cook," I said, laughing.

"Okay, I need to talk to you before you leave," Goddess said.

I handed Hope to Mina and went to talk to Goddess. I know that she is going through her own shit, but I know that she has been making time to go and check on Kai. I know that when you have an addiction that is something that you have to deal with forever. Going to rehab and meetings and shit doesn't make it just go away. I honestly don't know how Gotti deals with it in the business that we are in.

"I know that you are still trying to wrap your head around everything that has gone on with Hope, but Kai's cousin died today. He was shot a few days ago, and she is really going through it at that house all by herself, K," Goddess said.

"I'll go see her," I said as I got up to leave.

That's fucked up her cousin got killed, but right now my only concern is Hope and Mina. It's because of Gotti and Goddess as to why she's in my house, but right now that is all that I can do for her. Kai fucked me up when she up and quit returning my phone calls and then to know that she went back to that nigga. When Hope asked to call her, I had to act like I didn't hear that shit. I don't think that I could ever fuck with her like that again. I know that Goddess means well, and she genuinely does care, but right now, I don't have time.

I made my way out, and Mina and Hope are already waiting in the car. I'm ready to finally go fucking home, shit. Bri has Quita in a safe place. Well, she ain't safe, but she ain't going no damn where. I'm going to make her sit and think about what the fuck is about to happen to her for a while. Hope fell asleep in the back seat, and Mina is on her phone texting somebody. I'm not going to tell her right now, but that that apartment shit ain't gone happen no time soon. I'm not fucking ready, and her ass ain't either.

As I pulled up to the house, I see Envii and Gotti's cars are here. I hope Envii doesn't get on my damn nerves tonight, but I know that is asking for too much dealing with her. As we walked in the house, Hope woke up. Mina is just happy to be home, and not at Bri's. I just want to make sure that she and Hope are happy and good.

When we walked into the living room, Envii has it filled with balloons and gifts for Hope. She is a muthafucka, but she does have a good heart if you are on her side. Emanii is here with her, so she shouldn't get too crazy tonight. Hope ran up to Gotti and bypassed Envii. Hope loves Uncle Gotti and E. We all sat in the living room just kicking it and watching TV.

"Let me holla at you right quick," Gotti said, walking by me.

I followed him to the kitchen I know it's about to be some shit. I can tell by the look on his face that something else is wrong now. If we could just have one good day, I would be happy.

"Goddess is on some bullshit, K," Gotti said as I walked into the kitchen.

"What's going on? I thought she was getting help," I said.

"She is. It's not that. Mike is sick, dying, and she is talking about she needs to go see him to get closure," Gotti said, leaning up against the counter.

"Damn, what did you say to her?" I asked.

As Gotti went the fuck off, I can't even imagine no shit like that. I wouldn't be able to swallow that shit. Mike is this nigga that Goddess use to fuck with before Gotti, but that nigga is a sick ass nigga. I don't think that Goddess is trying to fuck with him or no shit like that. I'm trying to tell Gotti that, but he ain't trying to hear me.

I can hear E talking in the other room and Envii threatening him. I know that this shit got Gotti fucked up. He really loves Goddess, and he changed everything when he got with her. I don't have any advice to give that would help because my answer would be fuck no yo ass ain't going. I know that Gotti already has said that and much more. E made his way into the kitchen. Gotti finished up telling me that he was thinking about killing Mike faster. I can't believe that he hasn't killed him before now.

"Are you going back home?" I asked Enforcer as we all walked back into the living room.

"Fuck no he ain't coming back home!" Envii screamed.

E is my mans, and I know that he and Envii are going through something, but I want him out of my house. I don't like people living in my house. He has more than enough money to go and live somewhere else. He is only here because he knows that Envii is going to find out where he is and show up there showing her ass. She won't do that shit over here.

"I just came by to celebrate Hope's birthday since I wasn't invited to Disneyland," Envii said, picking up Hope.

"Thank you Envii. We appreciate it," I said.

"K, I'm about to go to the mall with Modesty," Mina said, trying to hurry up and get out the room.

"No, you're not. We'll go tomorrow," I said.

I can hear her stomping up the stairs, but she'll be okay. She is technically an adult, but I don't give a fuck about any of that. That's what she'll be trying to argue and say in a minute. We bout to have a whole bunch of family time whether her ass likes it or not.

"I just saw yo stupid stepmom," Envii said, playing with Hope.

KAI

"Are you ready Kai?" Goddess screamed up the stairs.

"Yes, here I come right now," I said, putting on my coat.

Goddess came over to go with me to Dink's funeral. This has been a really awkward situation to deal with. The crazy thing is yes, Dink is my cousin, but we have never been close. My grandfather and his grandma are brother and sister. Everyone is saying that Deontae shot him. The only people I have talked to are my aunts Lisa and Audrey because the rest of my family and me have been having issues since the night Dink got shot, especially my cousin Dina, Shod's sister.

I'm thankful that Goddess is going with me because Audrey isn't going. My Aunt Lisa is, but she is the type of person that tries to be neutral. I haven't told her what happened between Deontae and I because I can't tell her any shit like that. My Aunt Audrey knows what happened as well as Katrina and Cariya, but that's it.

Goddess and I made our way out the house and got into the car. I looked over to see Big Face starting his car. I'm getting sick of him and Ace. They aren't in the house they just sit in front of the house all day and night. I was relieved when I heard that K got Hope back. He hasn't called or came by, and I haven't tried to call him either. I don't know what to say.

As we get closer to the church, I keep feeling like I should have stayed my ass at home. I wanted to come because Dink is still my cousin and we were once close. We grew up together, but over the years we just lost touch. I'm not going to be here long, so it doesn't even matter how some of my family feels about me being here.

Goddess and I got out the car and made our way into the church. I see my cousin Dina standing by the door, but I'm not about to argue with her. We have already had words regarding Dink being shot and who the shooter is.

Dina looked me up and down as Goddess and I walked past her. I see my Aunt Lisa sitting with the rest of the family, but Goddess and I sat towards the back of the church. After going through the shit with Deontae and Memphis, Goddess has been here for me. Even Envii, she just has to constantly start with her smart-ass comments, but I have to say she ain't said one thing that I didn't need to hear.

The funeral finally started, and I'm relieved so that this can hurry up and be over. Where I'm sitting, I can see a clear shot of the casket that is close enough for me. I'm not going up there. Dink's mom and grandma keep looking back at me but haven't said anything. Goddess can feel that I'm uncomfortable because she keeps asking me am I ready to leave.

"Where is Deontae?" Where is the gun at?" Dina asked, walking up on me.

She caught the attention of several people in the church because they are looking in our direction trying to see what is going to happen next. Dina and I have never been close. She is older than me, and her kids are closer to my age than she is. Dina is the cousin that is always in jail or getting put out of apartments. She has no job and no car but always has so much to say about everybody else.

"Dina, I don't know where the fuck he's at," I said, shooing her away with my hand.

My hand motion was a warning that I'm trying not to fight her in this funeral, but I will. She just got to cause a scene like this is making anything any better. I already know from my aunts that she been going around telling people that I need to go to the police station and talk to them. I don't know what the fuck I would be telling them about a murder I know nothing about. This is the life Dink chose to live. Yes, he is my cousin, and it's fucked up that he is gone, but when you live by the gun you, there is a chance that you are going to die by the gun. I'm not going to the police station for a muthafucking thing.

Dina continued to yell, causing a bigger scene. Goddess and I got up and made our way out going the other way. I know that Dina is going to follow me and that is exactly what the fuck I want her to do today. All the shit that I've been going through and now this. Goddess keeps trying to pull my arm going in the other direction to the car, but I'm not going anywhere until Dina catch this fade.

I took off the blazer that I'm wearing and handed it and my purse to Goddess while she is begging me to just get in the car. I took off the heels that I was wearing and threw them down on the sidewalk and rushed Dina. We both fell in a bush, and I'm on top of her taking all the shit that I been going through on her face. Dina is short, brown skin with scars all over her face from popping pimples, and she these big ass bifocal glasses. She is thin, and her cocaine use has a lot to do with it. Her hair is short and broken off bad.

Surprisingly, nobody broke up Dina and me. As her nose busted and blood splashed all over my face, I thought about stopping, but not yet. I got off Dina and dragged her by her legs, down the hill in the church parking lot with her face scraping the concrete. The more she screamed, the more I wanted to make sure that she never forgot this shit. With Dina being my first cousin, you would think that she would be on my side instead of doing all the shit that she has been doing.

Nobody but Goddess followed me to the bottom of the hill. I wish Goddess would have stayed up there. I let Dina's legs go, and she attempted to get up. I kicked her in her stomach, and she fell back to the ground. I grabbed Dina by her head and banged her head into the concrete. She keeps digging her nails into my arms. I pulled my razor out my mouth that I knew I would be using today and cut Dina from her right ear to her left. As she started holding her face as blood started to gush out.

"Get in the fucking truck," Kamal said as he pulled up beside us.

33

Goddess handed me my stuff, and I got into the truck with Kamal. I have been wanting to talk to him since he showed up Goddess' that night, but today I do not want to talk about anything that we have been through. My phone started ringing. It's my aunt. I just let it ring I don't have shit to say.

The entire ride was quiet. K didn't even have any music playing. The ringing of both our phones was the only noises being made. He was ignoring calls, and I didn't even bother looking at mine.

We pulled up the house, and I jumped out the truck and ran into the house. I need to jump in the shower and start on my homework and get my mind off this shit. I put my phone on do not disturb and turned on the shower. As I got in the hot shower, tears started to fall down my face, and I promise myself that these will be last tears that I cry. I have to take back control. Most of this shit I brought on myself and Envii is right. I was fucking dumb. Tomorrow when I get out of school, I'm going to see K. We need to talk and get it over with.

* * *

"AHHHH!" I screamed out after I was woken up out of my sleep by Kamal calling my name walking to the bedroom.

"Damn, my bad," Kamal said, laughing.

My heart is beating so fast, and he scared the shit out of me. Ace nor Big Face came in the house. I know when I finally decided to go to sleep it was after one o'clock. I grabbed my phone off the nightstand it's 4:05. He damn sure could have waited until the sun came up for this. Kamal sat down at the foot of the bed, and I sat up and leaned against the headboard.

"Kamal, I'm sorry. I know that I fucked up," I said, breaking the awkward silence.

"I fucked up. I shouldn't have fucked with you like I did and brought you around my people so fast. I knew you were still stuck on that nigga," Kamal said, turning around to look me in the eyes.

"No, no it wasn't anything that you did. I should have talked to you. Just ignoring you and Mina was wrong, and I know that," I said, coming from under the covers and going closer to K.

I could feel that shit, and it hurt hearing him say that he shouldn't have fucked with me like he did. Kamal was everything that anybody would ever want. I had him, and I chose to go back to fucking with a bum all because of my insecurities with Quaneisha. Well, that and I didn't think that it was going to be something that would last. Yes, it was fun, and I was happy, but when you're so used to dealing with bullshit, it takes a while before you accept the fact that everybody isn't on that.

"So, what happened when you went back to fucking with him?" K asked.

I started off telling him about Memphis and what had happened when they fell out, and then I proceeded with telling him everything. As I got to the part about the miscarriage that started to fuck me up. It's something that I try not to think about. I act like it never happened. Just thinking about it and now telling K, I blame myself. K grabbed me and put me on his lap. No matter how hard I act like it didn't happen, and the only people I ever told before tonight was my Aunt Audrey, Cariya, and Katrina. I got myself together and finished telling K everything that happened at the house with Deontae and Memphis.

K hasn't said anything. He just is holding me with one arm and rubbing me with his free hand. I don't think that K and I will ever be able to be back like how we were. I wouldn't trust me if I were him, and I don't blame him for that. Him letting me be here and making sure that I am good from a distance is more than enough. I'd be lying if I said that I wanted him to let me go or leave.

K's presence this morning is needed, and I don't know what is going to happen with us going forward. He must still care because if he didn't, then he wouldn't have come and got me from Goddess' house. He wouldn't have put me up in this house and have his niggas sitting outside around the clock watching me. I'd have my ass back in Cherry Creek Greens. K softy moved my head from his shoulder and looked into my eyes, but still hasn't said anything.

"I'm gone be real with you. You're going to have to patient with me. If I didn't care about you wouldn't be here, but I'm going to need some time," K said still rubbing me.

"I understand."

"If you're standing beside me, I'm going to always have you and make sure you're good, but I need to know is this what you want? I'm done with this back and forth shit. So, what's it going to be?"

GODDESS

As I sit outside of the Love & Care Hospice Center, I'm debating on if I should go in or not. I told Genesis that I was going whether he liked it or not. He doesn't understand what Mike and I had for all of my childhood and until six years ago when I met Genesis. Mike is older than I am, and I started seeing him when I was thirteen. He was always around bringing me and my mom black. My mother didn't care what I did even at thirteen. So, me fucking the nigga that was keeping her high was right up her alley.

I woke up one night, and my mother had stuck a needle filled with heroin into my arm. My mother use to offer Envii and I black and everything else all the time since we were like ten, but we both always declined. After my mother stuck that needle in my vein, I was hooked. Mike was the one that would make sure I was high. I never had to steal, work, or anything else I just had to stay with Mike, and I would be able to stay high.

As I went to turn off my car and finally go in, I looked up, and Envii is tapping on my passenger side window. I'm not opening the door for her. *How the fuck does she even know that I'm here?* Envii hates Mike more than Genesis does.

"Bitch, you know I'll bust yo window. So, why play with me?"

Envii screamed loud enough for everybody in the damn building to hear her.

I unlocked the door, and she jumped in still screaming about how Mike wasn't ever shit. I know how Envii feels, and when I decided that I was ready to get clean, Envii was the one that was there with me and supported me. Envii is only three years older than me, but she was forced to grow up way quicker than I was. The first time I got clean was right after high school. I checked myself into rehab on my seventh birthday.

"Bitch, be real. Why are you here?" Envii asked, waiting for an answer.

At one point, I did love Mike, but I learned that being in a relationship with Mike wasn't what was best for me. When I stopped using the first time when I was with Mike, he didn't, and that is the reason why he is close to death's door now. Even though I was fighting every day to stay sober, Mike would be in the other room using, and Envii knows all this.

"Envii, you don't understand. I know how you feel about Mike, but I was with him for over ten years," I said.

"Let's be real. That nigga is old enough to be yo fucking grandpa. He was fucking raping you! You are supposed to be so damn smart. All the money I paid for you to go to school!" Envii screamed.

"Get the fuck out my car," I said.

"Nope, I'm not, so now what?" Envii said, turning her whole body towards me.

As I said, Mike is older than me. I was thirteen when I started seeing him, and he was forty-two. Now I'm thirty-two, and Mike is sixty-one. Unlike Envii thinks, I know now that I shouldn't have been sleeping with Mike. If you grew up like we did with all the dysfunction and bullshit that went on in our lives, some shit just becomes normal to you. While Envii went on to live somewhere else, my mom pushed me into farther into the arms of Mike to keep us both high.

I know that Envii means well because I know her. She has done a lot for me, and I know that she is worried about my sobriety just like Genesis is. Envii just has another way of showing her love and support, which if you don't know her, can be hard to understand. I know to get Envii out of my car, I'm going to have to fight her, and I don't have the energy to do that today.

I have been arguing with Genesis ever since I mentioned coming to see Mike. I don't want Mike. I love Genesis, or else I would still be with Mike. The way that I left Mike wasn't the best way I could have gone about it, and I just wanted to see him to tell him goodbye.

"Alright, if you're done looking at the building, start up the car so that we can go get something to eat," Envii said.

"What about your car?" I asked.

"That is why I have workers. I want some Benihana's," Envii said, dialing one of her worker's numbers.

I'm not going in with Envii attached to my hip. She'll be screaming the man is a rapist to everybody in the damn building. I'll just have to come back. I need to go and check on Kai and make sure she's okay. I'm glad that Genesis got there when he did to help her. I just wish that she could find the strength that she needs to keep going. I'm searching for that strength myself.

* * *

As Envii and I walked out of Benihana's, my phone started to ring, and it's Genesis. We haven't said one kind word to each other in two days. I answered the phone praying that nothing is wrong. With the life that Genesis lives, I know that there is always a possibility that something could be wrong. When the phone rings late at night, it scares me if Genesis isn't at home. I don't know what I'd do without him.

"Gionni is in the hospital. They're saying she has Lupus," Genesis said.

"Okay, do you need me to do anything before I come up there?" I asked.

"Yea, call Maci. I don't trust these muthafuckas," Genesis said.

Genesis gave me all the information that I needed to give to Maci, and we hung up. Envii nosy ass insisted on knowing what the fuck was going on. I called Maci while pulling out of the parking lot so that she can meet me up there if she isn't already there. Giordan, Gionni's mom, and I don't have a relationship. I have tried to be cool with her and have stopped Envii from jumping on her more times than I can count.

Gionni wanted to go with her for the weekend, and that is the only reason why she isn't with us. I wish I had time to get rid of Envii before going to the hospital, but I don't. I need to go and make sure that Gionni is okay. Envii is on the phone giving somebody orders. I really wish that my sister would leave the game just as much as I want Genesis to. I don't think Envii ever will. She loves it too much. The euphoria that she gets from the power she has is something that only the game can give her.

Envii and I got out the car at the emergency room entrance, and Giordan is sitting outside on a bench talking on the phone. I didn't waste my time speaking to her. I made my way inside the hospital. Envii just had to talk some shit to her, or she wouldn't have been able to sleep tonight. You can't take her anywhere because she does not know how to act.

As we walked up on Gionni's room, I can hear Maci talking. Envii and I made our way into the room. I went over to Gionni's bedside while taking in everything that Dr. Maci is saying. Genesis doesn't trust really anybody. He has a tough time believing that the sky is blue unless he sees it himself.

Genesis is dark chocolate and heavy. He is tall and has dark, sad eyes and a perfect smile. To the streets, Genesis is Gotti, hard and will set fire without hesitation, but for me, he isn't that. He is loving, caring, and supportive husband. Dr. Maci let us know that she would be back to check on Gionni and made her way out of the room.

I can tell by the way that Genesis is looking at me that he is still mad about me wanting to go see Mike. That I was then that would have been a problem too if I wouldn't have told him. He does a lot of things that I don't agree with, and my love for him hasn't changed.

"How are you feeling?" I asked, scooting my chair closer to the bed.

"I feel okay," Gionni responded.

"She is high as hell all that medicine they gave her. All the shit that she has had going on that we told her doctor about with her joints hurting, headaches, being tired and shit, all that shit is symptoms of this shit. She needs a new doctor!" Genesis spat.

I checked my phone because I know that it is getting close to time for me to go to my meeting. Envii is on the phone still giving out orders and still looking at me crazy. I know that Genesis told her that I was talking about going to see Mike. Genesis can barely sit in the same room with Envii for an hour before he wants to cuss her out, but he sure didn't mind calling her to tell her my damn business.

"I'm going to have to go in a little bit so that I can make it to my meeting," I said, and Genesis nodded his head.

Dealing with my addiction isn't easy for me to deal with, but I have been doing it for a while. It is even harder for Genesis to deal with. He never makes me feel less than or scolds me for it. I know that me starting to use again after I had been clean for fifteen years was crazy. When I heard about Mike, I didn't know how to deal with it, so I started snorting heroin. I was so high that I left some on my vanity in the bedroom, and that is how Genesis found out.

My sponsor Janice agrees with me that I need to go and see Mike to be able to get it out of my system for good before it's too late. Genesis isn't trying to hear any of that. When I heard that Mike was dying, I was surprised because I just knew that Genesis had killed him a long time ago. Genesis and I don't discuss his business, but I always make sure to listen and find out what is going on for my own protection.

I walked over to tell Genesis goodbye, and as we embraced, he whispered in my ear, "If you go and see Mike, I'm leaving" and kissed me on the check.

Genesis and I have never broken up taken a break or any of that. Since the day I met Genesis, we have been together, and there was no looking back. Hearing him say that caused my heart to fall into my stomach, and my mouth to fall open.

When I met Genesis, I was at the mall buying something for Mike for our anniversary. I was supposed to be buying something for Mike and was trying to figure out which pair of shoes and bag did I want. I picked out one of each I wanted and left the others at the counter. Genesis brought the ones I left on the counter for me, found me in the parking lot, and gave them to me. It was just something about him that made me feel like I had known him forever. It wasn't because he had money. At that point, I had my own money, and I didn't need a man for his money.

I had grown tired of being with Mike. He started off being the man with the sack and ended up being nothing but a dope fiend with nothing before it was all said and done. I never hung out with Envii and her people, so I didn't know that she was acquaintances with Genesis until I tried to introduce them to each other.

I hate arguing with Genesis, and when we do, it's never been this bad. Envii and I made our way out of the room. I have a lot to think about, and I'm sure my sister is going to give me her opinion.

GOTTI

"Who is that Gionni?" I asked.

Gionni isn't saying anything, but I know that she heard me. Some lady just came into the room and then walked right back out. Giordan jumped up and made her way out of the room behind the lady. I have been trying to be cool and not get crazy with Giordan in this hospital, but I don't know how long this is going to last. Being around Giordan irritates me, and I always end up going the fuck off. I'm up here for Gionni is what I keep telling myself. I'm just ready for her to get out of the hospital so that I won't have to look at Giordan.

I'm waiting for the doctor to come back and talk to us about some test results, and then I'm going to go and let Giordan spend some time up here. I have been back and forth up here for last three days. I'm tired, but I got some other shit that I have to handle. Hopefully, Gionni is getting out of here in the next few days.

Goddess is at work but texting me. She had better just keep her ass the fuck away from that nigga Mike, or I'm gone. I think what is really fucking with me is that after all this time she wants to see him all of a sudden. It wasn't a secret when I met Goddess that she was still with Mike. She was buying the nigga fucking gift when I met her. We never lied to each other about what we had going on with other mutha-fuckas. I'm not about to lie to nobody about shit. If I have to lie to you, then I need to get the fuck on and let you go. They say how you get them is how you lose them, and if she takes her ass up there to see Mike, I'm done.

"Who the fuck was that bitch?" I asked as Giordan came back in the room.

"What? What are you talking about? Giordan said, looking around.

"Giordan, don't play with me. I'll beat yo muthafucking ass in the hospital, and you know that."

Giordan light skin is turning red, so I know she's uncomfortable and thinking of a lie to tell me. This bitch lies about everything. I ask her how much something for Gionni is that she wants while she's with her and this bitch asks for thousands of dollars. If Gionni is with her on a school night, I'll ask did she do her homework, this bitch will lie and say yes and then the school's calling saying they're concerned. Gionni needed braces, I gave this bitch the money to pay for them, but until I took Gionni, she didn't get braces. I hate that I ever fucked her. If I could take this bitch back and keep Gionni, I would right the fuck now.

"Bitch, what is that yo girlfriend?" I asked, losing my patience.

"Yea," Giordan finally spit out.

I just shook my head and hoping this damn doctor will hurry the fuck up so that I can get away from this bitch. I don't give a fuck about this bitch having a bitch. I don't want her, and she should know that by now.

* * *

I PULLED up to the Benihana's to meet with Lady H. She called as I left the hospital asking to meet with me right away. I don't usually meet her alone, but I talked to K and E, and she just wanted to holla at me about something. The bitch is crazy, but her shit is always right, so I don't have any complaints.

As I walked in, I see Lady H sitting at a table all the way in the back. The chef is preparing her food, and she is on the phone talking to somebody. That surprises me because I have never seen her talk on the phone. We don't say very much to her on the phone, and she will go the fuck off if yo phone starts ringing during a meeting. As I sat down, she wrapped up her call.

"How's business?" Lady H asked and then took a sip of her water.

"Business is good, no complaints."

"Good, good. Glad to hear that. I have a proposition for you. I know that you have been doing what you do for a while now. Have you ever thought about making a change?"

Her question has me a little puzzled. *Is she asking me about leaving the game doing something in one of her businesses?* I told the chef what I wanted, and he started making it. Lady H's phone started ringing, and she ignored the call.

"It depends on what type of changes we're talking about," I said.

Using codes, Lady Heroin asked me to take over gun distribution for her organization. I wasn't expecting to hear that. I wouldn't be the one actually driving them. I would be the one overseeing that everything is being done properly. Shit, that is what the fuck I'm doing now is watching muthafuckas. I haven't been on the block in a long time. Accepting this would mean that I would be gone from home a lot more. Right now, with this shit going on with Goddess, I don't know if that is a good idea.

"Can I get back with you on that?" I asked.

"Of course, take your time. What else is going on, Gotti?" Lady H asked.

"Shit, dealing with my daughter. She's sick," I said.

"Lupus?" Lady H asked.

I looked at her a little curious how the fuck she knows that. There wouldn't be any reason for E or Kurupt to be discussing Gionni with her. She can tell that I want to know how she knows. I can tell by the way her facial expression changed.

"There's no easy way to tell you this, but we have been led to believe, I'm guessing for the same amount of time you have, that Tasia Gionni Thomas was my son Truth's daughter," Lady H said.

"What the fuck?" I said.

As Lady Heroin talked explaining to me everything the way that she is talking and all the information that she knows, I know that she isn't lying. She knows too much and has too much proof for this not to be the situation. I'm trying to take all this in, but the thought of Gionni not being my daughter is really fucking me up. Lady H pulled up pictures on her phone throughout the years of Gionni and her son. All the money that I have been giving Gionni, this nigga Truth has been giving her just as much. I got to fucking take a DNA test for Gionni, and she's thirteen.

As Lady H continues to talk, I'm responding and listening, but I can't believe this shit. I know that Giordan isn't shit, and for the first few years of Gionni's life, I financially was there, but I kept my distance because of everything that Giordan and I had been through.

When Giordan was like three months pregnant with Gionni, one night she wouldn't stop calling me, but I was busy. She kept leaving messages and shit going off, but I wasn't rushing to get to her. I was handling business. Giordan has always been a muthafucka when she doesn't get her way, so she just kept on calling. The next thing I know, the next morning that bitch had called the fucking police on me and all types of shit. She told them shit that I knew she had to be the one to tell it because it was shit that I had discussed in her presence.

After that, I couldn't fuck with her at all. For the longest, I wouldn't be around Giordan at all. I had Envii or somebody else pick up and drop off Gionni because I didn't want to be around that bitch. I wanted to kill her bad, but I decided for Gionni's sake I wouldn't. Now I'm thinking that I should have gone with my first mind and got rid of that bitch back then.

In one of the pictures, I noticed the girl that came into the hospital room earlier. That bitch was lying. That girl was Truth's girl. I'm not surprised. I just never imagined going through nothing like this.

As we ate, Lady H agreed to set it up so that Truth and I can sit down and talk. We haven't ever had words with each other. I know that we are going to have to eventually sit down, and he needs to know that regardless of what the results are that Gionni is my daughter. It's some shit that you just don't do, and this is one of them. I let her live when she called the police on me, but I never trusted her again, and this right here just shows me that I had good fucking reasons not to.

I paid the bill, and Lady H and I made our way out of the restaurant. A black Maybach pulled up, and Lady H got in. She rolled down the window, and I ensured her that I would be in touch about the new position. As Lady H drove away, I called Goddess. I need to talk to her about this shit with Giordan. She isn't answering. I've hung up and called back like six times now. She always answers her phone for me no matter where the fuck she is at.

I made my way to Love & Care Hospice Center. She had better not have her ass up here, or we are going to have a fucking problem. I had never had a time when I needed Goddess to be there for me, and she wasn't. Right now, I need her more than I probably ever have, and she isn't answering the fucking phone.

I am always here for Goddess. Everything that she wants to do, I stand ten toes down with her to do that shit. When she came to me and told me that she was sick of making the people that she worked for rich, and she wanted to do her own thing, I knew that it would be risky for her to get into her own advertising firm, but I stood by her and made that happen because that is what she wanted. Goddess doesn't agree with the life that I live, which is understandable considering her addiction, but this is all that I know. She knew what it was when she got with me. The only time we usually get into it is something about my business.

Now we have to go through this shit about Mike. As I got out of my car slamming the door, it caused the white lady parked next to me to damn near jump out the car. I don't give a fuck about that. I scanned the parking lot on my way through the door looking for Goddess' car, but I don't' see it. She already knows how I feel about this, so there is a good chance she is in another car or had somebody bring her ass here.

The lady at the front desk gave me Mike Washington's room number, and I made my way down the hall to see him. I had seen this muthafucka a few times when Goddess and I were together. This muthafucka is a rapist. How the fuck could he think that it was okay to be fucking Goddess when she was thirteen years old. I hate her fucking momma, Vivian, because she convinced her for years that the shit was okay.

I pushed open Mike's door, and he is sitting in the corner in a chair looking out the window. Nobody is in the room, but him. I looked around to see if I saw anything that Goddess would have left behind, but I don't. Mike hasn't said anything, and neither have I. The only reason that I haven't killed Mike is because he is my mother's baby brother. In our family, we never discuss the shit that should be discussed. This muthafucka fucking with little girls should have discussed, but it wasn't.

I've never told Goddess that Mike is my mother's brother because as far as I'm concerned, he ain't shit to me. As I was getting to know Goddess, and she told me everything about Mike, it wasn't hard for me to believe. I just think about the good chance that Goddess was not the only little girl that this muthafucka was fucking with.

"She isn't here," Mike said, breaking the silence as I opened the bathroom door.

I didn't bother saying anything back to him. I know that he has been in his feelings about the fact that Goddess left him. When he started using heroin, he fell off hard and never bounced back. When I was a kid, he was that nigga. But now as I look at him, he ain't got shit. What he did have, it left when Goddess did.

"How do you think it makes me feel that my nephew took my woman?" Mike said.

"I don't give a fuck how it makes you feel. You were fucking raping her. She was thirteen years old. What type of man are you?" I screamed, causing the window in the room to shake.

Mike, didn't answer my question and didn't have anything to say. The wrong words would have got him killed faster than he is already dying. He was supposed to be dead three days ago.

I told my mom about Mike when Goddess told me, and she, for whatever reason, doesn't want to believe it. I think that she knows that it is true and that it is something that she already knew, but black people will sit next to uncle so and so knowing he a fucking child molester. I'm not with that shit, and I make sure that Gionni knows what the fuck is and isn't okay when it comes to that because if not, then she could end up in a fucking situation like Goddess.

KURUPT

I walked into the warehouse where Quita has been for the past five days. I can smell her as I walk in the building. I don't know what the fuck Envii gave the authorization to do whatever she wanted to do in here, but as I walk up on Quita, I can't even tell that it was her. I wouldn't recognize her if it wasn't for the fact that she has on the same yellow shirt she had on the day at the hospital. Envii handed me a mask.

"She been eating?" I asked.

"Yea, what the fuck you said to feed her," Envii said.

Hope said that while she was with that lady that she was making bread and water. So, that is what the fuck she been eating for five days. As I can see, a lot of that is all over her shirt and the floor around her. Envii brought what I had requested to be here over to me and sat it down by my feet.

Quita is standing on her feet but has restraints on her ankles and arms. A thick belt is wrapped around her waist, which is used to control the restraint that she is in. I can tell by the fucked up way she is standing that every time Envii got mad about some other shit, she just came in here and pulled them all in different directions.

"I'm sorry, Kamal. I'm so sorry," Quita managed to say.

"Why did you do it?" I asked.

"You got another girl playing mommy to Hope."

I pulled out my machete and started to cut Quita, making as many cuts as I could. I pulled her restraints to position her where I needed her to be to make sure that I made as many cuts as possible. Envii has her in here in her panties, so I started cutting her legs the same way I did with her upper body. The more she screamed and begged, the more I cut. She could have stayed where she was at, and I wouldn't have given a fuck. When she involved Hope into this shit, she knew the consequences.

I picked up the container that has sulfuric acid and started to pour it onto Quita, making sure to pour it directly in the cuts so that it can get to her bones quicker. I pulled the chains to make her stand up straight, and she continued to try to squirm and move all for her to get no damn where. Her excuse that she had for taking my baby is bullshit.

Envii walked up to me and whispered in my ear letting me know that something we have been waiting for is ready, so I have to make this quicker than I want to. As the acid started to eat her body away fast, I filled Quita with bullets until she stopped moving and made my way out.

*　*　*

"MINA, I TALKED TO TYCOON TODAY," I said as we rode down the street on our way to the house.

"Who is Tycoon?" Mina asked.

"Mina, I already know. You don't have to keep lying. I don't understand why you feel that you have to lie in the first place."

Tycoon approached me today when he came into the shop with Lady H. He wanted to tell me how much he cares about Mina. Mina is a good girl, and I know one day that she is going to find somebody that loves, respects, and treats her how she is supposed to be treated. I know that Tycoon ain't that nigga. He has been giving his momma, Lady H, hell for a while now. I'm not going to tell Mina what to do when it comes to him or try to stop her from seeing him because if I do, then it's just gone make it last longer and be more bullshit.

"I can't tell you nothing because you always be tripping, and nobody won't fuck with me because they're scared of you," Mina said.

"Why would you want to fuck with a nigga that is scared of me in the first place? Tycoon ain't scared?" I asked.

"No, he's not scared of you," Mina said convinced that was the truth.

Tycoon is a bitch, but she is going to see soon enough. I got somebody watching her, but I haven't told her, and she hasn't noticed. Mina keeps telling me that I am too hard on her, and I be tripping over everything. I'm listening to everything Mina is saying, but I know that this shit ain't gone last long. I don't care how much likes him. Tycoon ain't shit. He is his dad's son, and he was a bitch too that swore he was that nigga.

"Are you back fucking with Kai?" Mina asked.

I know that Mina felt some kind of way went Kai went missing on us, and I know that if I tell her that she is three blocks away, that will be a problem too. Mina acts like she doesn't know what is going on, but she listens to conversations that I have, so I know that she already knows the answer to her question. I'm not about to go there with Mina tonight.

"That is why I'm moving out," Mina said as she slammed my truck door, waking Hope up.

Unless she plans on moving with Alice, she doesn't have anywhere else to go. She doesn't have a job and has no money other than the money I have given her, so I'm not worried about her going nowhere. She is used to living with me, so she wouldn't last in the house with Alice. Tycoon is still in fucking training, and he ain't even been off the porch, so he can't move her any damn where.

I'm not bringing Kai around until I know for sure that it is a good idea. The way Mina slammed my damn door now is not the best time. Kai has been cool the past few days. She says that she is ready and wants for it be us again. We will see if that is what she really wants. My people have been in the streets looking for Deontae, and they haven't been able to find him, but I'm about to bring em out. After this, I'll see if Kai means what she says.

As we made our way in the house, I can hear E screaming at Envii. Her car isn't outside, so they must be on the phone. They need to go see a fucking marriage counselor because I can't take too much more of this shit. Mina wants him out of the house. He starting to get on her nerves, so they are going to have to figure some shit out.

I know Mina is in the kitchen, so I made my way through the house to go and find her. Even though we just left from eating dinner, I knew this where her ass was going to be. I know that Mina was madder than I was when the shit with down with Kai, so I understand that she's not over it yet. I'm not going to lie and say that I am over it, but she needs to relax and just let me handle it.

"Mina, I'm about to go out for a minute, I'll be back," I said as I opened the icebox to get a water bottle.

"You going to see Kai?" Mina asked.

"Naw, do you know how much a car door costs?"

"What? What are you talking about?" Mina asked, getting irritated.

"Then don't slam my fucking door again," I said going upstairs to get Hope ready for bed.

I have to go out tonight. I have somebody I need to meet. Nobody needs to know what I am doing but me. I don't involve Mina in my business if I can help it. Some shit she needs to know so that she can understand why it is important for her to listen to me. Hope is so tired that she can barely keep her eyes open. I'm just happy that she is home. I don't know what the fuck I would have done if something would have happened to her. I got Hope out the bath, put her pajamas on, and laid her on her bed.

"E, you ready?" I yelled as I came down the stairs.

"Yea, why you want to go to the club? Nigga, you don't even like the club," Enforcer asked.

"Because I need to meet somebody, nigga, come on. I'm not staying until they cut the lights on," I said as we made our way out the door.

I really hate the fucking club, and I don't want to go, but I know the girl I need to see is going to be there. I saw her at the mall when I took Mina and Hope yesterday. She told me this is where she will be. The way this nigga E is driving it's not going to take long for us to get downtown. My phone started vibrating. It's probably Kai.

It's not. It's Kyra asking me am I at the club yet. I told her I was pulling up. E loves the club. He loves being in the spotlight and attention from the bitches and making as many niggas as mad as he can. That is just not my thing. I would rather stay at the house.

We jumped out and made our way out the car and up to the line. As we made our way past all the people standing in line, I see Kyra. I grabbed her hand and pulled her in front of me. Kyra is pretty. She's chocolate, thick, and has long straight hair. She is cool, but she parties and drinks too damn much for me. I can't deal with that shit.

We made our way into the club with her friend Ciara, and E was already all in her face. We made our way over to the table that I had reserved. I sat down and checked out what was going on in the club. A waitress made her way over to the table with bottles and Kyra grabbed one out of the bucket before the waitress could set it down on the table. She sat on my lap and took the bottle to the head. I bobbed my head to the Jeezy song that is booming out the speakers.

My phone started vibrating, and this time it's Kai, I got Kyra off my lap and my way outside so that I can hear her. I've still got Ace and Big Face watching her, so I know she's good. I've been trying to answer when she calls. I still don't know if I can fuck with her like that, but we'll see what happens. It's all on her at this point because I'm not about to beg her or nobody else to fuck with me. The phone stopped ringing by the time I got outside, so I called her back.

"Wassup Kai?" I asked as the call connected.

"Nothing, I'm bored. Are you coming over?" Kai asked, sounding sad.

"I don't know. I'm out with E. If I don't come tonight, I'll come by in the morning."

I know that wasn't what she wanted to hear, but she made shit the way it is. I was all for us, and she made her decision so, she must do it the way I want or no way at all. I know that she is bored and lonely being in that house.

Kai's family has still been on some bullshit since her cousin got killed. I know that is fucking with her because they are accusing her of knowing where the gun is and all types of shit. The police had picked up that nigga Deontae and only had him for three days that is why I wasn't able to find him. They let him out and dismissed the case without prejudice, so they can go and get him at any time. I have to get to that nigga before they come and get him again.

"Well, I'll let you get back in the club. Have fun," Kai said.

"Alright," I said and disconnected the call.

As I walked into the club, I see Kyra standing on the couch, and her whole ass is out in this tight, burgundy, short dress that she is wearing. I walked up on the table and looked at her, and she jumped down and put her ass in the proper place. I'm all for having a good time and if you want to party do that, but I'm not about to be out with no female doing too fucking much. I'll be happy when this shit is over.

"Hi, K," a woman said from behind me.

I turned around, and it's Katrina, and Cariya is with her too. I spoke, and Cariya is shaking her head. I know that they know that Kai is in one of my houses, and I'm sure they know everything else that has been going on. Katrina said some smart shit under her breath and walked away. I don't owe either one of them an explanation for a damn thing that I do. They should have been telling Kai not to do what she did, and this wouldn't even be going on.

"Who is that?" Kyra asked.

"Nobody," I said, pulling her closer to me.

I'm sure E is leaving with that bitch because ain't no bringing no random hoes to my damn house. He knows that, so we don't have to have that discussion. The later it gets in here the more lit these muthafuckas gone get.

"You ready to go?" Kyra asked.

"Shit, yea you ready?" I asked, jumping up.

"Yea, my head hurts," Kyra said.

As we made our way out of the club, I saw the reason why Kyra was ready to go, and it wasn't her damn head hurting. Her baby daddy is in her with another bitch. I had my arms around Kyra's waist as we walked out the door. E is behind us with Ciara drunk ass. He is holding that bitch, but only to keep her from smacking the ground. We made our way to E's car, and Ciara's car is parked farther down the block. E threw me his keys and made his way down the street.

Kyra told me where she lived. She lives in the Cherry Creek Greens where Kai used to live. I made way over there. As Kyra and I talk, I see that she doesn't really know what she wants to do. It seems like she doesn't have any type of plans for the future. She just had a little girl that is only a little over a month old, and if nothing else motivates her, that should.

"Are you coming in?" Kyra asked as I pulled into the entrance of the apartments.

"Naw, I'm going to go home, sweetheart. What are you doing tomorrow?" I asked.

"Nothing, my daughter is going with her dad, so I'll be here by myself," Kyra said rubbing my dick.

"What time?" I asked.

"Two o'clock."

"I'll be over at 1:30," I said, kissing Kyra on the cheek.

KAI MORAE

Somebody is knocking on the door and ringing the doorbell. I'm running downstairs wishing it was K, but I know it's not. I don't know who the fuck it could be. I looked out the window, and I don't know whose Audi this is unless Ace or Big Face has a new car. I opened the door, and it's Mina. I don't really know what to say because I know she was mad as hell at me the last time we saw each other.

"Hi," I said, breaking the silence between us.

"Wassup, I need to talk to you," Mina said, brushing past me and making her way in the house.

Envii was supposed to be coming over, but that was a few hours ago. Something must have come up. I followed in behind Mina as she led the way to the living room. K hasn't told me anything about what has been going on with Hope and Mina. When I ask about them, he is really short and just tells me shit like their good.

"Are you just using my brother, or are you really trying to be with him now?" Mina asked as I sat down on the couch across from her.

"I was never trying to use your brother, Mina. I want to be K, but I know that I have to wait until he's ready now because he doesn't trust me," I said.

Admitting that to Mina and saying it anybody is a hard pill to swallow. I have never been the girl that a nigga wasn't able to trust and count on. The fact that K doesn't trust me and is keeping me at arm's length fucks with me, but it what it is. I know how Mina feels about her brother, and he can't do any wrong in her eyes. Mina's phone started ringing, and she answered it.

I got up to check my phone to see if K has called me. I find myself checking my phone every five minutes to see if he has called or texted me. I'm trying not to blow him up, but this shit ain't easy. This having a piece of him shit ain't working for me. Shit, it's not even a piece as far as I'm concerned. If I call, he usually answers, but he'll come by and will be back out the door before we finish an episode of *Martin*.

Mina is definitely on the phone arguing with a nigga by the shit that she is saying. I know how K is when it comes to her, so I wonder if he knows about this nigga. I doubt it the way he acts. He wants Mina to live with him for the rest of her life. If he lets her go to the mall with Modesty, she'll be lucky. Mina ended her call with her boo.

"Kai, I need a favor," Mina said.

"What do you need?" I asked.

Mina blew hard and looked up at the ceiling. "I need you to tell K that I'm pregnant."

I was not expecting that one. She must not know that I'm damn near an outsider and that I don't have the weight that I used to hold when it came to K anymore. I know that she doesn't want to tell K, but I can't help her with this one.

"Mina, K and I aren't on the best of terms right now," I said.

"K still fucking love you, or you wouldn't be here in this fucking house," Mina said as the doorbell rang.

"Mina, you're eighteen. It's nothing that K can do about it," I said, getting up to let Envii in.

"I'm nineteen. You missed my birthday when you went back to that broke ass nigga. But Kai, I need you tell him it's by Tycoon," Mina said now begging me after throwing my shit in my face.

Out of all the niggas in the world, of course, she starts fucking with the plug's son— not the son that has his shit together, but the son that is always in some bullshit. Mina had told me about Tycoon, and I knew they were dating, but she didn't want K to know. I never said anything to him about it. I have heard K and Enforcer talk about all the bullshit that he does. Instead of just playing the back where his momma wants him to be, he insists on being seen and making a name for himself. As I opened the door for Envii, the way she brushed past me stomping, something is wrong with her ass too.

"I can't believe this bitch ass nigga! What the fuck are you doing here? You don't like her no more, remember?" Envii screamed, looking at Mina.

Envii turned around looking at me for the answer while Mina was shaking her head and mouthing at me not to tell Envii. Envii got back to cussing and yelling about Enforcer. Ever since the first time I met them, they were arguing. I don't know how the fuck you stay with somebody that you are arguing and fighting with all day every day.

"What did he do now?" I asked since she hasn't said what he did yet.

"That muthafucka brought me a teddy bear, balloons, and some fucking shit from Victoria Secret!" Envii spat, rolling a blunt.

I'm just trying to think what the fuck did he do that was wrong. Mina is looking at Envii crazy, and my phone started ringing, so I jumped up to get it damn near tripping over the rug all for it, not to even be K, but fucking Katrina. I'll call her later and when Envii isn't around.

"Damn, bitch. Is K still tripping with you? I've never seen you move that fast," Envii said in between taking pulls from her blunt and laughing.

"Fuck you, I don't understand why you are tripping with E because of him buying you shit," I said, taking the heat off my ass.

"This right here is not teddy bear and balloons pussy. I don't know what type of pussy you have, but this ain't that!" Envii said, tapping her pussy.

"You just be tripping just because you can," Mina said.

Envii continued to go off, and I just don't understand what the issue is still. She just likes to act crazy for no reason. Her birthday is not even today. It's not until the end of the month. My phone started ringing, and it's my Aunt Lisa, so I answered. I haven't really talked to her much since the funeral, other than a text here and there. I know that she is mad about what happened between Dina and me.

"You have mail over here from a bail bonds," Aunt Lisa said.

"What?" I asked confused.

I shouldn't have any mail from a bail bonds. I don't know why all of a sudden, they would be sending me mail. I know she saw Deontae on the front page of the paper and news like everybody else. I know that she thinks that I am still fucking with him even though I have told her that I wasn't over and over again.

I told my aunt that I would come by and get it later. As she talked about what has been going on in the family, I keep thinking about the letter from bail bonds. I finished up talking to her as Mina started talking about K, so I got my aunt off the phone, so I can know what's going with K.

* * *

As K PULLED up to my Aunt Lisa's I jumped out to grab my mail out the mailbox she put it out here for me to get. That is her way of saying she doesn't want me in her house because of what is going on with Deontae. I'm starting to question whether he killed Dink or not because if he did then why the fuck did he get out. As I made my way back to the truck, I busted open the envelope from the bail bonds.

*Ms. Smith, you are in default from your payment arrangement and now owe 500,000...*was all I needed to read. Any of the rest of the shit in this letter doesn't matter. How the fuck do I owe them this? I never signed a bond for this much money.

"What's wrong?" K asked as I got back in the truck.

I handed him the paper. I know for a fact that I didn't sign for him to get out. I haven't talked to or seen him since the night I left the house with Gotti. Before they dismissed the charges for the murder, he was out on bond. I don't know how the fuck he could have come up with that type of money. None of his family have that type of money, but clearly, he found some of it from somewhere and some-body signed my fucking name on the paperwork.

"Don't worry about it. I'm going to handle it," K said, rubbing my thigh as he pulled out of my aunt's driveway.

"How?" I asked.

K didn't say anything he just looked at me.

I don't have that type of money to pay, and K shouldn't have to pay for that muthafuckas bond. If I say anything else to K about it, it's just going to start some shit I know. We had a good night. We went to dinner at the Cheesecake Factory. I'm starting to feel like we are getting somewhere now.

"Will you come in?" I asked as we pulled up to the house, and Ace pulled up behind us.

"Naw, I got to go handle something. I'll call you in the morning," K said, kissing me on the lips and unlocking the doors.

"Are you fucking with somebody else?" I asked.

"Naw. Who told you that Katrina or Cariya?" K asked.

I just looked at K, but I didn't respond to his last question. They both told me that K was at the club with Kyra. *If you are fucking with that bitch, then why the fuck am I living in this house and driving yo fucking car. I could have gone back to my apartment and figured some shit out if this ain't going no damn where.* I wasn't going to say anything because of everything that has already gone down between us, but not saying nothing about what the fuck is going on is where I went wrong the first fucking time.

"It's not what you are thinking, Kai. I don't want that bitch. I'm taking care of some shit," K said.

"What could you be taking care of that involves you fucking with Kyra? I already went through this shit with her and Deontae. I'm not going through that shit with you," I said as I got out and slammed the truck door.

I made it to the door and struggled to put my key in the door. K came up behind me and opened the door. I tried to walk fast to get the fuck away from him, but he grabbed me. Him fucking with Kyra would explain why the fuck he can't stay here. I tried to be understanding of the fact that I fucked up, and that is why he doesn't want me at his house around Hope right now. We didn't discuss anything about it being okay for him to be fucking with Kyra in the meantime. Out of all the bitches out here, he just had to start fucking with her.

"Kai, I'm not fucking her. I don't give a fuck about that bitch. Do you hear me?" K said, still holding me from behind, preventing me from moving.

I didn't say anything. I don't know what the fuck to think. What the fuck else could it be if he ain't fucking her. Why the fuck would he lie about being at the club with E and that bitch in there on his lap. K didn't say anything else. He removed my hair from my neck and started to bite and kiss my neck, just hard enough to hurt but still feel so damn good.

K slipped his left hand in my pants while still holding me with the right. I'm so wet that I know it's a wet spot on my pants. As Kamal, continued to kiss, lick and bite on me and play with my pussy, I can't help, but moan out, and this is just his fucking fingers. K pulled my pants off me with my back still facing him and went back to playing with it, as we walked towards the stairs the stairs. Before I could reach the third step, K stopped me.

"Fuck this shit, I'm not waiting to get upstairs," K said, turning me around and pushing me down on the stairs.

K ripped my panties off and dove head first. As K, flicked his tongue on my clit, I wrapped my legs around his head and started to grind on his face leaning back with my elbows on the stairs above me. The way that he is sucking out my soul, I don't want him to ever stop. The way that he is going, he 's not stopping any time soon. As my legs started to shake, K kept going.

I came, and K ate it all up. K picked me up and carried me upstairs. The way that K is kissing me, I have never been kissed before. The way that he is touching and rubbing every part of my body leaving no part of me deprived is something that I have always yearned for.

As K, laid me on the bed, I just prayed that he wasn't this gentle with my box. I laid back to watch as K came out of his clothes. His body is so right like he lives in the gym. K's chest is coved in tattoos and has no room for anything else. K stepped out of his boxers, and my mouth dropped as I look and his fat, long, and perfect dick. It has to be the biggest dick I have ever seen. Shit, I'm scared and so ready for it at the same damn time. K made his way on the bed and stopped at my lips below to give her another kiss, causing my body to shake.

K kissed his way up my body while using those wonderful hands of his roaming all over me. Every touch is making me want this even more than I already do. K kissed me as he made his way inside of me, causing me to gasp for air as he filled me perfectly. With each stroke that K made, he took more than he already had. My legs are on his neck, and he pushed them to the headboard, going deeper than anybody ever has ever been.

Just as I wanted K to quit making love and fuck me, he started. With one leg on his shoulder and the other in the air, K beat my pussy with just enough pain and so much pleasure. K continued to work my pussy, and I threw it right back. I came, and K is still putting in more work than I was expecting. I wanted to scream out, but my mouth is so dry, and the only thing wet and making noise is K and my drenched box. I've never been this wet, it's never been this right, and I've never cum so many times.

K flipped me over on my stomach with so much force, but I don't give one fuck. With each thrust, I can feel all of him as he punished my pussy for my foolish ways, but I don't mind at all. All the worries that I had have all gone away the way that my pussy is leaking. With K pulling my hair and slapping my ass, I throw it back like only I would do for him.

"O, myyyyy goooood K, right there!" managed to escape my lips.

"You like that shit, yellow? Take it," K said, not missing a stroke and hitting my new spot.

K came releasing all of his seeds inside of me. As we both tried to catch our breath, I want some more of this East Side Gangsta. I started playing with his beautiful masterpiece and got it right back like I wanted it to be and jumped on it backward riding him like a porn star. As I ride K, slide up and down getting loose, and fucking K like he fucked me. I spun around on the dick with it still inside of me, held onto the headboard, and proceeded to do my muthafucking thing. The way that K is moaning and groaning only made me go harder.

As I bounced up and down on the throne, I can feel myself again. I'm finally in the place that I deserve to be with the man that I deserve that has given me more than any man has. As I start to get tired and start to roll on this killa dick, K starts to beat me from the bottom. I'm not letting him win this round, so I got up on my feet and started to bounce on his dick like I am on a pogo stick. As K started to moan, I did too as I came again. K flipped me over with on leg on his shoulder as he kissed my ankle and the other on the bed. I can't take anymore, and K proceeded to give me all the life I needed.

KURUPT

I need to get up, but I really don't want to. Kai is laying on my chest, and I want some more of that, but I have to go and handle what I was supposed to be doing last night. I'm not telling Kai, what I'm doing because I 'm not trying to involve her in any of this, but her part that she is going to have to play is coming real soon. Little does she know, I'm not fucking Kyra and have no plans on fucking her. She's not my type. I just need to pretend she is for a little while. I know she didn't sign the bond for that nigga to get out because she ain't went nowhere without my niggas watching her, and whoever the fuck signed her name spelled it wrong. She was so fucked, up looking at the amount they said she owed, she clearly wasn't paying attention to that.

"Kai," I said in between kissing on her.

"Yea," Kai mumbled, turning her head in the other direction.

"I have to get up and handle some shit, and I'll be back," I said.

Kai didn't budge or move she just kept laying on me. I would love to lie here all day, but I can't. I have to go. I looked at the clock, and it's almost noon. I moved Kai onto the bed. I jumped up and threw on my clothes. I have to run by the house and get dressed and get out here.

As I made my way down the stairs, I can hear my phone going off at the bottom of the stairs.

Just like I knew, Mina's been calling and so has Kyra. I called Mina back, and of course, she didn't want shit but to be in my damn business, so I hung up on her. I made my way out the door, and Big Face is sitting out here. I nodded my head to him as I jumped in my truck. I plan on getting this nigga Deontae today, so this watching Kai shit will be over real soon.

"What's up?" I asked as the phones connected.

"I been calling, what happened to you last night?" Kyra asked.

"I got caught up with something I had to handle."

"What you doing right now? You got the baby?" I asked.

As Kyra told me that her baby daddy would be pulling up shortly to get the baby, I thought, *fuck I don't have time to change my clothes*. I've got Kai's juices all over my damn shirt. The nigga seen me over there and didn't say shit but started tripping with her over the phone as soon as he walked out the door. I need to get this nigga before he goes in the fucking house. Broad daylight, I don't give a fuck I'm not about to keep waiting and finessing. Now is the fucking time. I'm sick of pretending to like Kyra. I want to kill her too because she's fucking irritating just like a rat bitch.

I hit the highway and made my way to Kyra's. Mina's name popped up on the dashboard. I answered, and she is coming through the speakers of my truck screaming at Hope.

"I'll be there in a minute. Quit fucking yelling at my baby and in my damn ear." Ace is watching Mina and Hope, but Mina is asking for shit from the store. I told her I would go and get it, and E walked in the house. I hung up on Mina. E can go and get it.

I pulled up to Kyra's so that I can wait for this nigga to pull up. My momma started calling, but I'll call her back later. All she wanted to talk about is me sitting down and talking to Krack with her. If she wants to forgive the nigga and be his damn friend she can do that, but I don't have time for that shit right now.

I checked the clock, and it's now 12:50. I texted Kyra and asked had Deontae come to get the baby, and he hadn't. He told her he didn't have a ride and that bitch doesn't have a car. I hit the steering wheel and made my way home. I don't have time for this shit. I'll get him later, but I'm not going to sleep until I get that nigga.

* * *

I'M SITTING a few houses down from Deontae's momma's house. A few people done came and went. I'm guessing those were his sisters, and I'm waiting for this other lady to come out and then I'm going in to get him. I texted Kyra, and they're both still waiting for a ride to bring the baby to him. All I could do was shake my head at both of their bum asses.

The lady that I'd been waiting to come out is at the front door. Whoever the fuck she is she's been in there for three hours. Everybody else was in and out. From what Kai told me nobody in his momma family really fucks with her because of how scandalous she is. She sure got a lot of fucking company. Deontae's in there because he came out on the porch to holler something to one of the light skin bitches that left out of there. The last visitor pulled out the driveway and made her way down the street. I jumped out of the car and made my way to the door. It's almost midnight, so hopefully, his fucking momma is sleep. If not, then her ass is going too.

I have on all black and a ski mask. It's cold as fuck out here, so that ain't going to alarm nobody but whoever opens this fucking door. I knocked on the door, and it swung open.

"Damn, what took you so long to get here?" Deontae asked as I hit him across the face with my nine, causing him to fall to the ground. I shut the door behind me and walked over him. His punk ass ain't going nowhere too fast.

I walked through the house and saw the lady that I'm guessing is his momma nodding in a recliner chair about to fall out. I see a bottle of pills sitting next to her, so she done took so many of them she not waking up no time soon. I know that she pops pills from Kai, so I'll leave her ass alone. I made my way back to the front door where

Deontae is still laying holding his bleeding mouth. This nigga really is a bitch.

"Who else is in here?" I asked, pressing my heat under his chin.

"Nobody just my momma. Please don't kill my momma," Deontae begged.

"We'll see how I feel after you're dead and then I'll decide. Nigga, you don't get to make no demands," I said, pushing him back to the ground.

I called E and told him to meet me at the spot. I would have called Gotti too, but I know he still dealing with the shit with Gionni and Goddess. I have been trying to let him be until he's ready. I told Deontae to get the fuck up so that we can get the fuck out of here. He managed to get up, and I knocked him back to the ground. That's how the fuck he was doing Kai when he had her in that fucking room holding her hostage. He wanted to see me, so here I am.

"Nigga, get the fuck up and get ready to walk. This will be the last walk you ever take, nigga, so appreciate it," I said ready to go now.

As we made our way out of the house, this muthafucking nigga started crying. I really don't want to hear this shit. When we got to the car, I popped the trunk, hit him with the butt of the gun, and threw his ass in the trunk. I don't want to hear no grown ass man cry. I tied him up hogtie style.

I have to make one more stop before going to the spot. In order for Kai to show me that she really fucks with me and this nigga doesn't mean shit to her after all that he has done to her, she is going along for the ride. I called Kai, and she answered before I heard the phone ring good one time.

"Damn, did the phone ring? You miss me?" I asked.

"Shut up, yea."

"Throw on some on some clothes. I'm about to come and get you."

She didn't ask any questions or have anything to say, which surprised me. I talked to Kai as I made my way to go and get her. I pulled up, and she ran out and jumped in the car. As we rode to the spot, we didn't say anything to each other. I turned up the heat in the car because Kai was bouncing in her seat. I know that she's cold. She always fucking cold. I reached over and grabbed Kai's hand while keeping my eyes on the road.

We pulled up to the spot, and I jumped out and made my way over to Kai's side to open the door for her. She got out and grabbed me. I pulled her in closer, and we went into the building. I tossed Dirt and Bad News the keys on the way in so that they can get Deontae and bring him in.

As we walked in the building, E and Envii were standing in the middle of the floor, but they aren't arguing which surprised me. Envii has a confused look on her face. I know she is wondering why Kai is here. I am very serious about keeping those I love and hold close as far away from the streets as possible. But, the only way that I will know that Kai is really down with me like I am with her and not just saying the shit because she thinks that is what I want to hear is how she plays this situation.

The time that Kai and I spent apart, I learned that she didn't tell me everything that she was doing when we were not together. I know that she was selling dope for her cousin. I also know that she was serving my momma. As soon as Kai went missing, my momma told that. I don't blame her doing what she was doing, but she could have fucking told me.

"Girl, what are you doing here?" Envii asked. I know that shit was killing her not to know.

Kai looked up at me waiting for the answer to why she is here. Dirt and Bad News finally brought the reason inside the building. Dirt and Bad News woke up Deontae and made him stand on his feet without their help. Kai looked back and forth between Deontae and me twice, waiting for me to say something. I'm watching how Kai is looking at him and seeing if I see any love still there. She's still squeezing my arm and hasn't let go running to the nigga's aide, and she isn't concerned about the bruises on his face or his busted nose.

"Do you love me?" I asked Kai, loosening my grip on her.

"Yes," Kai said, looking up at me and stepping back from me.

"How much?" I asked.

Kai walked up on Deontae unzipped her coat and pulled out a gun.

Where the fuck did she get a gun from unless Enforcer didn't empty that house out like he was supposed to. I looked back at him and Envii. He is shaking his head no and holding up his hands, so if he didn't leave a gun there, then how else did she get it?

As I went to turn around, Kai started to shoot Deontae.

"Hey, Goddess tells me all the time I have the right to bear arms. Since we are the only ones without a record, I had to take her to get licensed. It's only right she gets her revenge," Envii hollered in between hitting her blunt.

I know that Yellow has been through it with this nigga. As she continues to empty the clip after this nigga stopped moving, I know that she needed this. We will be having a talk. She can continue to be the police and let me handle this shit in the streets after this. I walked up on Kai as she continued to pull the trigger, even though the clip is empty, and he has been gone. As tears started to roll down her face, I proceeded to kiss them away while trying to pry the gun from her tight grip.

"It's over. He is gone, Kai," I said as I proceeded to kiss her tears away.

Envii is yelling and screaming at Enforcer. I held Kai tighter as she continued to wet up my hoodie with all the tears and pain falling from her eyes. I promise myself and her that she will never feel this pain again. I promise to have her all the way and never to let anybody come in between us again. Envii is giving me the worst headache that I ever had in my life with her fucking yelling about a damn teddy bear that nigga. Enforcer better take his ass home.

GOTTI

I let myself into Giordan's house. Gionni is at school, and when she gets out, Goddess is picking her up, so I got some time. I made my way through the house, but this bitch ain't here. I'm not going anywhere until she gets here. Regardless of what the test results come back, I'm going to always be here for Gionni. I just want some fucking answers, and I'm going to get them today.

Shit is finally back to regular business. Kurupt has everything under control. I have been able to make sure that Gionni and Goddess are good. Goddess is working on staying clean, and Envii has been staying at the house with us. Envii makes me want to get high as I can be. So, I don't know how the fuck she is going to help her. I checked the time, and I've been here for twenty minutes, and this bitch ain't made it here yet.

Somebody is at the door putting a key in. Giordan's bitch ass walked in with both of her hands filled with shopping bags. I once found myself being all for this bitch and giving her more than I have ever given anyone before her. There is almost nobody walking this earth that I hate more than this bitch now. I let her live because of Tasia Gionni and only her. The fact that this bitch thinks that it is okay for her to lie to me and another nigga has me hot.

"Bitch, take another step, and I'll kill you right now!" I spat as foam started to form in my mouth.

Tears started to form in Giordan eyes, but I don't give a fuck about them. She has cried many tears over the years, and I have never cared about any of them. She started shedding tears after she fucked up and tried to play me. Gionni keeps popping in my head and is the only reason why I haven't sent this bitch to hell where she belongs.

"You dumb ass bitch. Why the fuck would you try to play me for all these years?'" I asked.

I wanted to pull my gun out, but I don't need to this bitch feels me more than she ever has with me still sitting on the couch. Giordan started stumbling over her words as I told her to shut the fuck up. Nothing she can say is going to change the situation. Nothing is going to heal the pain that I feel in my chest. As bad as I don't want to take a DNA for fear of what the test might read, I know that it has to be done. I jumped off the couch and walked up on Giordan, pulling out my heat and forcing it into her mouth, breaking her front two teeth in the process. Right now, I don't give a fuck about much.

"If Gionni comes back not mine, on my momma nigga I am not only going to kill you, I'm going to kill everybody in your family," I said and spat on this hoe like the trash she is.

I pulled my heat slowly out of Giordan mouth as her bottom to teeth dangle. I yanked my heat out roughly pulling them muthafuckas out to join the teeth that are scattered throughout the living room floor. I am getting ready to do some shit that I never imagined having to do, but it needs to be done so that I can sleep better. With each step that I make to my car, the harder I know this is going to be. I haven't said too many words to Goddess since she told me that she needed to go and see Mike. If I never needed my wife, I need her now. As I ran every stop light that isn't green, the madder I become. The hatred that I have in my heart right now for Giordan is worse than it has ever been.

I pulled up to the house not seeing Goddess' car. I jumped out and made my way through the house only to not find my wife. From the first day that I saw Goddess, I knew that she would be mine. When I found out that she used to use dope, it made me love her more than I ever did. It made me want to save her and protect her from that shit. The time when I need her more than I ever have with my shoulders feeling like I have the mountains on them, she is nowhere to be found. I made my way to the theater only to find Gionni and no Goddess.

"Where is Goddess?" I asked.

"She said she was going to the store, but she has been gone a long time," Gionni said in between smacking on her popcorn.

"Come on, Gionni. I need you to ride me right quick," I said, which are the hardest words that I have ever said.

I can feel tears forming that is causing my eyes to burn. I pushed them back as Gionni, and I made our way out of the house. We got in the car, I called Goddess, and I got no fucking answer. It went straight to voicemail. As Gionni jumped from the way I hit my steering wheel, I realized that I have to keep it together for her. She has no idea what is going through my head. The pictures of Truth and Gionni start to take over my mind as I swerve in and out of traffic.

No matter what these test results say, I know that I will never love Gionni any less and never treat her any differently. After I put my pride to the side and started to be in Gionni's life, she has been what has kept me going all these years. The streets can take a toll on you and be a burden at times, but Gionni's face that resembles my mom's has kept me going and with my foot to niggas necks for so long.

"Who is Truth, Gionni?" I asked.

"Umm, what? I don't know," Gionni said as she started to swarm in her seat.

"Gionni, you can tell me the truth. I won't tell your mom about this," I said.

Gionni started to cry, and the sight of my baby girl crying her eyes out made me feel so bad. As Gionni started to tell me all about Truth and his family, my heart broke. As she started to describe the way that Giordan would beat her and make her promise not to tell Truth or me about each other, just made this even harder. I wiped the tears away from Gionni's eyes while ensuring her that she did nothing wrong. I reached over to hug Gionni tight, letting her know that my love her will never change no matter what.

Gionni took her first steps with me. She said her first words with me, and no matter what, my love will never change. I got myself together as Gionni and I made our way in to be tested. The longer Gionni continued to cry, the worse I felt having to take her in here, but I needed to know the truth.

"Baby girl, I promise no matter what, I am going to always be here for you. Please stop crying, Gionni. This is not your fault. You did nothing wrong baby, I promise," I said as we made our way to counter. Tears started to fall from the lady at the desk eyes.

I have killed some niggas, and I have made some niggas and bitches suffer, but this is by far the hardest thing that I have ever had to do. As I look in Gionni's eyes, I know that I have to stay strong for the both of us. Honestly, right now, we are all that we have. I tried to call Goddess again and still nothing this time it did ring. When Goddess told me that she had been addicted to drugs, it caught me by surprise. It was something that I never expected from someone so beautiful and gentile. I have been as supportive as I could be throughout the years and to find out that she is back using makes me feel helpless.

The technician started to swab Gionni's mouth, and all I can do is pray that these results come back saying that she is mine biologically. As the tech started to swab me, I know that I have to take this position with Lady H to escape my reality.

* * *

"WHERE THE FUCK HAVE YOU BEEN?" I roared, causing my words to echo throughout my home.

"Oh, my... Genesis, you scared me," Goddess said while gripping her chest.

I can feel her heart beating from across the kitchen. As she explained that she had a campaign that she had to oversee, the angrier I became. I never needed Goddess more than I did today, and she was nowhere to be found. As I made my way across the kitchen to the icebox, I can feel my blood pressure rising. I grabbed Goddess by her neck without thinking twice.

"I needed you today, and you were with that nigga. I know you were, so don't lie!" I spat.

"Geeeennnsis, I'm so sorry. What is going on?" Goddess said as I loosened my grip on her neck.

I let go and fell to my knees, wrapping my arms around Goddess's legs. I have never handled Goddess in this way, and I know it's only my pride that has allowed me to handle her in that way. I never have before and never will again. As I began to cry, letting all of the pain and anger inside of me out, Goddess fell to her knees and began to hold me. The protection and love that I feel in her embrace I have never felt before and am not willing to lose for my uncle. Fuck the family at this point because the only people that matter to me are Gionni and Goddess.

* * *

As I STIR in my sleep from my nightmare of Gionni not being mine, I feel the warmest and smoothest hands that I have ever felt stroke my shit. I opened my eyes and looked down at Goddess as she circled the tip like only she can do. As she swallowed me, all I could do was laid back and let her do her do her thing. Goddess spit me out, licked up and down my shit, and found her way to my balls. With each slurp that echoes throughout the room, I can feel the tension that is on my shoulders loosen up.

Goddess mouth is just too pretty, and so are her pink lips. I pulled her up and sat her where she belongs. As Goddess began to roll her hips on my shit, I began to beat her from the bottom. As my toes started to curl, I can feel myself coming, and I'm not ready yet. I rolled on top of Goddess and began to take out everything out on Goddess' box as her legs began to shake. I'm not letting up. I am not stopping until I want to.

Goddess is still shaking as I beat my box as if it is going to be the last time. I made my way down to my pussy and dove head first into home. The way that Goddess' legs are wrapped around my neck, I know that I am doing my job. As I flicked my tongue on her clit, I can feel that she is getting ready to come again. No NA and no sponsor can give Goddess the feeling that I am giving her. I'm not ready to cum yet, and as long as my wife is getting all of me, nothing else matter right now.

As Goddess came again, I continued to do my muthafucking thing. I licked her clit while working my finger in and out of Goddess, causing her to beg me not to stop. I asked her did she want me to stop as I came up for air still working her with my fingers.

"Noooo babbbby, pleeeeasee don't stop," Goddess begged as I got myself back to work, giving her the best that I got.

I flipped Goddess over on her back and continued to work her like I have never had. Goddess has the perfect arch in her back as I began to bring her all the down like she has never have been before. With every thrust I give, Goddess is throwing right back causing nothing but her soaked box slapping against my balls to echo throughout the room.

GODDESS

*a*s Gotti lay next to me snoring, my phone started to ring. I hadn't seen the number that popped up on my screen since I checked myself into rehab when I was a child, but I still know it by heart. My mother has caused so much pain in my and Envii's lives. I vowed to never speak to her again after she bashed me for wanting to get clean.

"Hello," I said with as much attitude as I can find.

"Goddess, baby girl, I am so happy to hear your voice," my mother Vivian said.

"What do you want?" I asked not losing the hatred that I have for her.

Imagine being woke up out of your sleep as your mother is pushing poison into your veins with a smile spread across her face. I never got the chance to be a child. I never got to go to homecoming or prom. All I got was a high and Mike. My mother gave me to Mike on a silver platter. I can remember him dangling a package over my head as he broke my hymen. I can remember me begging him to stop. The one gift that I had to give to a man that truly deserved it was taken by a man that didn't deserve it.

"Vivian, what do you want?" I asked, losing my patience as she continued to say how much she missed me.

"I need to see you, Goddess. I know that I fucked up, and I was wrong for everything that I did to you and Envii. I was in a horrible place in my life. Envii's father had left me, and I just didn't know what to do. I am so sorry baby, and I am ready to admit to the wrong that I have done," Vivian said.

I'm starting to feel sick to my stomach, and I'm about to be sick and I knew this was coming because I used yesterday. Chills form all over my body, and I jumped from the bed hoping to make it to the toilet. All I can do is pray that the vomit that I am holding my mouth does not touch the floor. As I vomited into this porcelain god, I feel Genesis gripping my hair and preventing it from getting wet. I can hear my mom screaming on speakerphone in our room. I'm sure that is what woke Genesis up.

As Genesis began to smooth the stray hairs that have fallen to my face with every hurl that I'm given, I know what I need to do. Unfortunately, Envii and Gotti are not going to be pleased, but I need to look my addiction head-on in order to be able to make it through the storm. The reason I started to snort heroin a few months back was when I had heard that Mike was not doing too good. A part of me feels like I am to blame for leaving him when I did.

Mike was never right for me. From the beginning and as time went on, even once I got clean, he continued to bring me down. The love that Mike gave me never felt right and always felt like it was forced. As I began to throw up again, Genesis began to rub my back as I got it all out of me. Genesis started running water in the sink as I came up after emptying my stomach. Genesis began to wipe my mouth with the warm towel. I always knew inside of me that it was something that would trigger me and make me start getting high again.

As Genesis picked me up off the floor, held me tight, and took me out of the bathroom, I can still her Vivian screaming out for me. I can feel in Genesis touch that he is getting mad, but he hasn't said one word. Genesis placed a warm towel on my forehead. As I began to reach around the bed for my phone, I finally found it, taking Vivian off of speaker phone as I can feel the heat coming from my husband. Genesis has never met my mother or father, and when we got married, I didn't invite either one of them.

As far as Genesis knows, I have never met my father. He is a person that if I never see again, I will die satisfied. The fact that my mother is still begging to see my sister and me and has yet to mention him lets me know that she is still stuck in his web.

"We will be over soon," I said as I hung up in my mother's face and began to shake uncontrollably. I am fienin' hard, and even with Genesis holding me, the cold chills have hit my body quick. Even with Genesis warm embrace, I still can't stop the shaking. Genesis began placing soft kisses on my forehead and face, and I am reminded of why I love Genesis so much and will never lose him no matter what.

* * *

"Envii, I remember. Even with how high I was, I still will never forget what Vivian did to us," I pleaded with Envii as she put out another blunt only to light another.

"I can't step foot inside of there. That will be worse than being in isolation, Goddess," Envii said and proceeded to take long drags from her blunt.

The pain that my sister has endured I can't ever imagine. Vivian stopped me from writing Envii while she was locked up. Vivian refused to go to court, which left Envii locked up way longer than she .needed to be. My sister used to be the sweetest girl ever and had so much love in her heart, but that all changed, and the streets are feeling that every time her feet touches the ground.

· As Envii paced the floor over and over damn near going in circles, I started to remember when Vivian would tell Envii to go into the basement because she thought she was better than us. I still can see the tears that formed in my sister's eyes the first time Viv sent her into the basement. Envii is so hard after being abandoned other than her communication with Lady H. Even with all that she won't dare let a tear fall from her eyes.

"Get yo shit and come on. You want to see this bitch, so we are going to see her, and if you step in front of me or try to stop me from speaking my mind, I won't hesitate to kill yo ass too!" Envii spat and then proceeded back to hitting her blunt like it would be her last.

As I made my way to the car, I remember finding the letters that Viv kept from me the day before I left for rehab. There were hundreds of letters with Envii crying out for help and begging my mom to come and get her. I can never imagine being put into a small windowless hole and seeing no way out. My sister spent more than half of the time that she was locked up that way, which was over two years in isolation. I can still see the wet spots on the letters from tears I knew that Envii shed. Envii is doing damn near a hundred making her way to Vivian's, and I am praying that nobody comes out into the street because if they do their dead.

I have never seen the rage that Envii has in her eyes before. My sister displays her anger by screaming, yelling, killing niggas, and cutting herself. We made it Viv's, and with each step that Envii takes into the house, I can tell that her legs are burning as the fabric from her True Religion jeans rub against it. Only Enforcer and I would know about the scars that are placed all over Envii's body in specific spaces that no one will ever be able to see. Envii kicked in the door, and I see some of the rage that is inside of her leaving her body. It is not all gone, and I know the conversation that is about to happen will only release more of it.

Vivian rose to her feet as her front door flew off the hinges. Envii made her way to the love seat crossing her legs and lighting another blunt. I know my sister is only self-medicating and has been doing so since she got home just to try not to feel the pain anymore. Tears started to form in Vivian's eyes as I sat across from Envii in an oversized chair, preparing myself to protect my sister. As Envii held my hand and sat with me as I went through treatment the first time, I started to feel the pain and regret come into my body. Why didn't I ever stand up for Envii and why was I so focused on getting high that I allowed my sister to starve.

"Bitch, you wanted to talk get to fucking talking!" Envii screamed so loud, causing my ears to ring and the windows to shake.

As the cold winter wind started to make its way through Vivian's place, I am still hot, and the tension in the room is hotter than hell will ever be. I can tell by looking at Viv that she is searching for the right words to say. I know that she has heard and seen some of the shit that Envii has done come across her old ass TV. It is the same TV that was here when I left. I can tell that it is on its last leg the way that the picture is coming in.

"I am so sorry to the both of you. I have made a lot of mistakes, and I know that there is nothing that I can do to make things right…" Vivian attempted to say as Envii rose to her feet like lightning ran through her.

"Do you? Do you know what the fuck I was going through in the juvenile as I sat in the fucking box! Do you? Have you ever felt like you are the only person in the world and nobody gives a fuck about you! Do you have any ideas how many nights that I can't sleep waking up thinking about that shit? Do you?" Envii screamed, forcing Viv to fall on the couch as Envii is in all of her personal space.

"Baby, I am so sorry. I made a mistake," Vivian whined as my father and grandfather made his way into the room.

Yes, you heard me right. Not only is Leonard my father, but he is my grandfather too. I have not seen this bitch since I left, and I prayed that I would never see him again. Every day when my bones ache, I am reminded of him. I was born deaf, but luckily Envii made enough money so that it is not visible to anyone that is not looking for small hearing aid I was able to get. Luckily, unlike many others that suffer from my condition, I don't have any physical genetic mutations.

When Envii and I were teenagers, I can remember him coming into our home when it was pitch black, and the only people up in our home were the roaches. He touched Envii and I in places that we should have never been touched and made his way into my mother's room. I can still hear her crying in between begging him to stop.

"Hey, baby girls. I am so happy to see y'all. Y'all have come to be beautiful young women," Leonard said, licking his lips as he kissed Envii's gun.

As tears started to form even faster in Viv's eyes, I can see the devil jumping up and down in Envii's as she pushed her gun into Leonard's mouth. As Leonard begged he had the audacity to say that he was just trying to make us feel good. As the thought of my grandmother appeared in my head, the thought that after he had his way over here, he found his way back into her bed started to make me feel sick. I have never seen Envii in action with her pistol, but the way that she is lightly bouncing from foot to foot I can tell that she is getting ready to.

"Bitch, you wanted to make us feel good! Are you fucking kidding me?" Envii screamed as she bounced from her left foot to her right foot sending bullets through Leonard's head.

The gunfire is so loud that I have to cover my ears and even with me doing this I can still hear the ringing throughout my hearing device. As Leonard's body smacked the ground, Viv's screams began to get louder while Envii let out a laugh from her gut that I know the neighbors can hear. Viv balled up into a ball scared of what is going to happen to her next as Envii continued to laugh, making her way over to her.

"Envii, please no don't do it," I begged as I jumped from my feet trying to get in between Envii's gun and Viv.

Envii will not even look me in the eyes, and it is like her feet are gorilla glued to the floor. The more I try to push her back she still hasn't budged. I'm not going to even try to touch her gun because I know my sister. Viv is begging, crying, and apologizing for everything, but I know with all the hurt that she inflicted on my sister, Envii doesn't care what she says. None of that matters.

"Envii, please. She is still our mother. Think about Nanny," I pleaded.

KURUPT

"Mina, how do you feel about Kai now?" I asked.

Mina started to text some damn body, making me mad as hell. Everything that I do I have Hope and Mina in mind, and I think about how it can impact them. I want Kai in this house, but I know that until Mina is okay with, it will never happen. Kai has shown me over the past month since she got rid of Deontae that she is all for me and only me. I don't want to go another night without her being in our bed.

"I don't care if Kai comes here, K," Mina said, looking up from her phone.

I know when Mina is lying because she will not look me in the eyes, but as she looks at me now, I know that she is telling the truth. I thought I was going to have to cuss Mina the fuck out to get Kai back in here, but that went smoother than I figured it would. Mina made her way out the kitchen with her ear glued to the phone. I snatched up my keys and coat and made my way to the door.

"I'm going to Kai's. I'll be right back!" I yelled up the stairs before making my way out the door.

Hope is already sleeping; she had a long day. I have made it a priority to keep a smile on hers and Mina's faces since I have had

Hope back. I'm going to do whatever it takes to make sure that their smiles never leave their faces too. They have been through enough and shed enough tears to last us forever.

* * *

As I PULLED up to the house that Kai is in, I can see that the light is on in the bedroom that she has been sleeping in. I hopped out and made my way to get Yellow. Since Yellow has been over here, she has been patient and understanding of how I was feeling. Now that I know for sure that she is down with me the whole way, I feel comfortable bringing her into my home.

Kai's family has still been on some bullshit and acting funny towards her, but that has only caused her to become closer to me and finishing her degree. I don't give a fuck about any of her family and have been drilling that into her head over the past few weeks. Fuck them! I know that Kai didn't have any communication with that nigga Deonte and him killing her cousin. I don't give a fuck if they ever realize it. As long as we got each other, fuck everybody else.

"Get yo computer and books and let's go home," I said as I walked into the bedroom.

Kai jumped up onto her feet, snatched her computer charger out the wall along with her phone charger, and made her way towards me. I'll have somebody come and pick up everything else. None of that shit is important. Kai and I made our way downstairs, her free hand locked into mine. My phone started to ring, and I don't give a fuck who it is tonight. The only thing that matters is that Kai is going to beside me when I wake up in the morning. The streets are going to be here when I wake up, and tomorrow I will get back to them, but tonight they are going to have to wait.

As Kai and I pulled away from the house as Anita Baker's "You Bring Me Joy" came through the speakers, and at this moment, I could feel her words more than I ever have before. Kai reached over and grabbed my hand as I bent the corner and held onto my hand tight for dear life like she never wanted to let it go, and I'm never going to let her go no matter what. Everything that has happened is in the past, and it doesn't matter.

I fucked up by not letting Kai know the real about Quan, and I have to accept my part in that. As much as I want to comfort her and every other woman in my life from the reality of my lifestyle, I need to have some conversation with them so that I can always feel comfortable knowing that they will never not be good.

As we pulled up to the house, I jumped out and made my way over to the passenger side to let Yellow out my truck, picking her up with her squeezing my neck tight and holding onto her laptop with the other. The feeling that I have right now feels so right that nothing can prevent me from feeling this way.

* * *

As I CAME up for air after diving into Kai's ocean again this morning, I have never had any female get as wet for me as Kai has. I have never felt somebody feel as right with me as Kai. As I kissed my way up Kai's body, my phone started to ring for the hundredth time. Kai started to kiss me as her juices fell from my beard.

"Kamal please call your dad back," Kai said, stopping me from slurping on her tongue.

As I laid my head on K's breasts, she started to tell me how she wished that she could call her dad. K started to tell me about her dad, which is something that she never has before. I just made my assumptions about him that he either ain't shit or is dead. Kai started to tell me about how when she was seven he caught a case, and she never saw him again. He was killed shortly after going to prison. As silent tears began to fall from Kai's eyes, I started to feel them pour onto my head.

I made my way up to Kai's face to wipe her tears. Seeing how this shit is still fucking with her, I promised Kai that I would talk to Krack, grabbing my phone to see what he has to say after all this time. I leaned up against the headboard as Kai rested her head in my lap.

"Wassup?" I said as the call connected with Krack.

"I'm glad that you called," Krack said.

I didn't say anything back because, to be honest, if it weren't for Kai, I would ever never called him back. I remember the rough days that I had when Alice kicked me out this muthafucka, he should have been there, but he wasn't. He was probably off having a family with another bitch. Meanwhile, Mina and I were going to sleep and waking up in hell.

Krack wants to meet up, and I agreed with Kai rubbing on my chest. It is probably best that we get the big issues off our chest face to face rather than over the phone. I told him to come to my house on Saturday, in two days, so that I can handle some issues in the streets that have been on the backburner while I tended to my family. Krack is going to have to be on my time. He agreed, and I disconnected the call as Kai squeezed me tight.

As I kissed Kai on the top of her head, I know that I am about to have to hit the streets hard like I never have before, but that is fine. I am ready, and I know that my foundation at home is solid enough to be able to still be here when I get home. My phone started ringing, and it's E, so I know that I have to get up and get ready to head out.

"Yea, what's up, E?" I said into the phone.

"I'm about to go downtown. I got the heat in the car, and they pulled me over because somebody called and said I had drugs in the car!" E spat.

"Alright, I'll call Iman," I said and disconnected the call.

"Call Envii, Yellow. E just got picked up," I said, getting up to jump in the shower.

If it ain't one thing, it's fucking another now this. I know it was nobody but some bitch he is fucking. No niggas in the street are calling the police saying that shit. E should be out in a few hours, but in the meantime, I need to go and holla at Bad News and Dirt so that I can check in on a few things E was supposed to be handling.

As I get out the shower, I can hear Mina screaming my name. I just ignored her ass and got dressed. She doesn't want shit important. When I'm here, I don't know who calls my name more, Mina or Hope. I'm sure it's Mina, and she don't be wanting shit that she doesn't already have or know where it's at. I don't want to deal with Envii, so that is why I told Kai to call her.

I got to get with Gotti to check on some shit. Out of all days for E to get knocked today had to be the day. I came out the bathroom, and Mina is the room begging Kai for something. I made my way down the hall to see Hope before I leave. She is sitting on her bed watching cartoons and didn't want to be bothered. I called Iman and made my way downstairs. It's probably Gotti at the door.

I opened the door while filling Iman in about E, and Envii had already called him. I ended the call with Iman and caught Gotti up as I made my way into the kitchen to get my keys. I can't imagine finding out that Hope might not be mine. That would be some shit that I wouldn't be able to deal with. Gotti is way better than me because Giordan would have been gone a long time ago.

"It's some more money on the floor from Lady H," Gotti said as I kissed Kai goodbye.

Gotti filled me in, but I can't believe that he would want to take that position with him having to be away from Gionni and Goddess. We headed to Gotti's truck as we made our way to peep out some shit that I been hearing about, but I wanted to see it myself. Bad News and Dirt have been telling me about this nigga Lee. I sent Brionna to go and see him, so after she does her part, I'm going to do mine.

As we pulled up to the corner store, I see Brionna on Lee's arm, and they are getting to an Impala.

"You see that nigga Jason," Gotti said.

I looked over to where Gotti was pointing and seen Jason in the cut watching Lee too. I shot Bri a text and told her to do this shit now. I can't wait, and some other niggas get to Bri. Gotti started following Lee and Brionna, and Jason went in the other direction.

All of this could have been avoided. Lee was working for us, but he can't seem to remember what his cut is. He has been sending his people to deliver the money, but it's never right, and Gotti can't ever seem to get in contact with him. We pulled up to the house, and Bri and Lee made their way in. I jumped out and made my way in, and

Gotti stayed in the car. I let myself in the house. Bri had left the door unlocked for me.

I got to give Bri some more time before I make my way upstairs. I waited a few minutes. As I made my way upstairs to get this nigga, I can hear Lee talking. I made my way to the room they are in and pushed the door open, and Bri is straddling Lee, she has on some lingerie shit. His dumb ass hasn't even noticed that I am in the room.

"Bri, I got it from here," I said as she jumped off Lee, grabbed up her clothes, and left the room.

"What the fuck? You dirty bitch!" Lee screamed.

"Nigga, what was our deal?" I asked, not that it matters now.

As he sat up and started to try to explain what his personal problems are today, I started to fill his body with bullets. I made my way out of the room and downstairs. As I went to turn the backdoor knob, somebody started shooting at me from behind. I turned around and started to bust back while opening the door. Walking backward, I still kept shooting until I got to the car.

KAI MORAE

*M*onica's "Everything" came through the speaker on my desk, and this song is exactly how I feel. It has been a month since I have been back in the house and things have been better than good. K is everything that I ever wanted, and I am happier than I have ever been. He is talking to his dad, and things are getting better with their relationship. He has been over here for a few hours, and his girlfriend is on her way over.

"Call 911, Kai!" K screamed from down the hall.

I jumped up to grab my phone from across the room where I put it so that I can focus on studying. I called 911 as I made it down the hall to the theater. Krack is lying on the floor grabbing his chest. I told the operator the address and explained to her what was going on while she gave me instructions. I followed her instructions while she insured me that the ambulance is at the gate. K is pacing the floor with Hope in his arms, and Mina is crying hysterically.

A few minutes passed, and the ambulance is finally outside. K left out to let them in, and I stepped back so that they can do their job before pulling Mina off the ground too. I just pray that he is okay for K and Mina's sake.

As they got Krack on the stretcher, Alice walked into the room. Alice had been begging K to talk to Krack, but we have recently found out that was so she could see him too. I know that K, didn't invite her over here, but every time he comes over, she just happens to stop by. Tears welled up in Alice's eyes as she hugged Mina. I left out of the room to go and check on K and get Hope.

Mina and Alice made their way out the house and to Alice's car. K is just standing outside the front door watching but hasn't said anything. I rubbed his back as Hope reached out to me. I told K that he needed to go and be there for his dad and he agreed kissed me and made his way in the house to get his stuff so that he can leave. Hope and I made our way in the house. The food should be done, so Hope and I can eat.

* * *

"YELLOW, I need to talk you right quick," K, said as my phone started ringing.

"Alright, I need to see who this is. I think it's the people about my internship downtown," I said, answering the phone.

It's somebody calling from downtown, but it damn sure isn't who I thought it was. It's Mina. Tycoon has been arrested, and they took her downtown. I know my facial expression has changed and that is causing K to be concerned and staring down my tonsils. I told Mina that I am on my way to get her, and K instantly started going off.

"What the fuck is going on? Where is she? She left the house with that nigga, and what the fuck did he do, leave her somewhere?" K screamed.

"No, Kamal is not like that he got arrested," I said like that was better, and he really started tripping.

I attempted to calm K down, but he really doesn't want to hear it right now. Finally, K started to relax and look around for his keys. I told him that I would go and get Mina because he didn't need to. I know that tonight is about to be a long night, Luckily Krack is doing better and is being monitored in the hospital, but now this. K agreed to let me go and get Mina, and I made my way out the house. As I hit the lock on my 2018 Lexus LS, Envii skirted into the driveway on two tires.

"Bitch, I need some advice I'm sure bitches come to you like Shirley all the time, but this shit is fucking with me," Envii said as she got out of her car.

"Come ride with me. I have to go and get Mina from the police station," I said, jumping in the car.

Envii started to tell me about some girl calling her and telling her that she was sleeping with E a few days ago. The way that she puts on this front that she doesn't care I know is bullshit because if she didn't care, she wouldn't be coming to me with this. Goddess must be busy for her to come to me. Envii and I have gotten close since I moved into K's. Envii took me to the shooting range and bought me a gun. That is her way to bond. She is going to talk some shit and not hold nothing back, but she has a good heart.

"What did you say to her?" I asked, jumping in before Envii kept talking.

"That I wasn't Barbra, and she ain't Shirley, so she needs to talk to him!" Envii spat.

"I thought everything was good, and he was back in the house?" I asked.

"No, he's not back in my house. He hasn't been staying at K's?" Envii asked.

I shook my head no as she started to dial someone's number, and I pulled into the police station. I jumped out the car while Envii cussed hitting my dashboard with her fist. They are always going through something, so this doesn't surprise me. I don't see how they have lasted together this long. They have been together since they were kid's doe and that history can't be easy to walk away from.

As I walked into the station, Mina rose to her feet and ran towards me crying with a box of tissues in her hands. I don't know what Tycoon has done to get arrested, but I know that it can't be anything good. From the way that Envii has talked about his mom, I don't see why he is still in custody. She should be able to come and get him without a problem. I got Mina into the car and jumped in the front seat so that we can go home.

"He ain't answering his phone. Where the fuck could he be at?" Envii said, not really asking.

Shit, I have no idea where Enforcer is. I hope he is isn't at Katrina's, but there is a chance knowing the both of them. Mina still has not told K that she is pregnant, and the longer she waits, the worse it is going to be. Now is really not a good time. Envii threw her phone into her bag and turned around facing Mina.

"What the fuck is the problem? His mom is not going to let him sit down there. What the fuck. Is for speeding again?' Envii asked.

"No, it's not that. They are saying that he killed somebody. They kept trying to show me pictures of Rico. Somebody cut his entire head off, put it in a bag, and put it on his baby momma's porch," Mina said, wiping tears from her eyes.

As I look at her in the rearview mirror, I don't really know what to say. I know how she feels about Tycoon. She has talked to me about him so much since I've been in the house, so shit, I feel like I know him and have never met him before. The car behind me started honking the horn signaling for me to go.

As the young nigga continued to honk their horn and talk shit, I started to hit the gas. Envii jumped out the car and ran up to the man that is behind me in a Honda Accord. She done pulled out her gun, tapping it on the man's driver side window. I jumped out the car to get her. We really don't have time for this.

"Envii, come on. We need to go," I said, trying to pull her back to the car.

"Bitch nigga, I will kill you and yo fucking momma. Don't play with me. If you're in a hurry, you should have left earlier!" Envii spat.

It's some young niggas in the car that is maybe eighteen, and they are begging and pleading for Envii not to kill them. They were just talking hella shit, but after Envii jumped out on them, everything changed.

Envii snatched away from me and leaned into the window and then made her way back to my car. Luckily, we are not far away from the house, so we made it back home fast since traffic is not that bad tonight.

Mina jumped out the car running in the house, and I already know that K is just as mad as he was when I left. He was in a good mood after he got back from the hospital, but I know that has all gone out the window now.

"I need you to ride with me," Envii said as she slowly made her way out the car.

"To go where? It's a lot going on over here as you can see," I said.

"Bitch, I got time. I just need you to be around in case I go to jail tonight. So, you can bail me out. Goddess can't," Envii said as I turned to go into the house.

As I opened the door, I can hear K screaming calling Tycoon all types of punk bitches and Mina screaming just as loud trying to get her point across. As I walked into the living room, Hope isn't down here, so she must be upstairs sleep. Mina and K have always got along so good and now this.

"He's my child's father. I'm never going to leave him!" Mina screamed.

"He's yo fucking what? What the fuck did you just say?" K asked.

"You heard me!" Mina screamed.

"Look at this shit, do you see that? That nigga ain't never getting out ever! He killed the mayor's fucking stepson with his dumb ass!" K screamed, turning on the TV and turning it up.

Envii started choking on her blunt as she sat down and started watching the news. As K flipped back and forth between all the news channels, it is on every station, and Tycoon's mugshot keeps popping up.

"Fuck you! I hope you fucking die!" Mina screamed and ran out the room crying.

"You want me to die! If I die who the fuck is going to take care of you and baby?" K screamed.

Envii jumped up from the couch with her blunt hanging from her mouth. "I got her," Envii said as she left out the room to go and check on Mina.

Who knows what the fuck Envii might say and if it'll be anything nice and comforting. K sat down on the couch and turned to ESPN. I sat down beside K and laid my head on his chest. It's nothing that I can say. He was going to have to find out eventually, but this isn't the way he needed to find out. Even though Mina is an adult in K's eyes, she will never be that, and I don't think no nigga will ever be good enough for her.

After seeing the pictures and hearing what the reporters had to say about what Tycoon is being accused of, he damn sure wouldn't be my pick for her. I just hope that Mina realizes it before it's too late.

"I tried to be nice to the bitch was even talking nice through the door, but she said fuck all of us, and we could all die tonight," Envii said as she walked back into the living room.

The alarm dinged letting us know that somebody is walking in the house Envii peaked her head down the hallway to see who it was. It must not be Enforcer because she's not cussing. K turned up the volume on the TV.

"K, I need to talk to you *alone*," Alice said, looking me up and down.

I'm not sure what the fuck that was for. I haven't ever done anything to Alice. Shit, at one point we were cool. She must have an attitude because Krack didn't want her at the hospital, but that doesn't have shit to do with me. I barely know him.

"Kai, I need you to ride me to finish getting the stuff for Emanii birthday," Envii said.

"Alright, here I come," I said.

I'm glad she said that because I don't want to hear K's mouth about being in bullshit with Envii. K and I discussed my past, and I promised that I would leave it there. I was surprised by his reaction to me serving Alice, but relieved. I understand after being around K the life that he lives, and I know why he doesn't want me involved in it as much as possible.

Envii and I made our way out of the house, and I just pray that we find him fast and I can go home. I have school in the morning. Envii turned up Boosie's "Retaliation" and skirted out of our driveway. Envii was there for me in her own special way while K and I were going through shit, and that is the only reason why I'm in the car with crazy driving bitch now, praying that I make it home in one peace as she weaves in and out of traffic.

GODDESS

*A*s I sit across the room from Mike, I can feel a lot of the pain coming from my body, and I haven't said a word to him yet. When I walked into the room, he started crying, and I just sat down across from him in one of the chairs. After seeing Viv and Leonard after all these years, I haven't been in my right mind lately. I have been getting so high just to be able to make it through the day. The fact that my eyes are not closed right now is surprising me.

"I miss you so much. I am happy that you decided to come and see me," Mike said, wiping his own eyes.

His daughter Melody came into to the room. Melody and I are the same age, and she hates me along with the rest of Mike's thirteen kids. Yes, thirteen, and all of them and they mommas have a problem with me. That was one of the reasons why I was tired and fed up with dealing with Mike. It took a long time for me to realize what Envii, Genesis, and everyone else has been trying to get me to see that what Mike and I had was wrong. No school books or professors could teach me that. I had to come to the reality of that on my own.

"Did you tell her?" Melody screamed.

"Melody, please calm down and stop yelling," Mike begged in a soft tone.

"Tell me what?" I asked as Melody walked out the room, slamming the door.

"It doesn't matter come here," Mike said, reaching out to me.

Just as I was about to say no and tell Mike how I feel about him the one person I did not want to know that I was here busted through the door. The look that Genesis gave me lets me know he has so much hatred and disgust for me right now at this moment. Genesis has always been so loving and understanding with me, but I know how he feels about Mike. I just knew that he would never find out that I came here. As Genesis made his way to Mike's bed and grabbed Mike by his neck, I rose to my feet.

"Genesis, no please stop he is already dying," I begged.

"Get the fuck off of me, you fucking dope fiend! I know he's my fucking uncle!" Genesis screamed, flinging me off his arm, causing me to fly across the room.

Genesis has never called me out of my name, and when it comes to my addiction, he has never talked about it in a derogatory way. He has always been supportive and doing everything that he can to walk with me during the challenge of me staying sober. *Wait a minute did he say that Mike is his fucking uncle?*

How could Genesis keep something like that away from me? Mike never took me around anybody. I never knew any of his friends or family. As time went on, I met a cousin here and there and few other people in his family, but never Nancy, Genesis's mom. I got myself off the floor as Genesis beat Mike until his face is full of blood, and I know that he is getting closer and closer to heaven's door. I am trying to get up off the floor, but I can't it's like no matter how hard I try I can't move, and I keep slipping back down to the floor. Then everything just went black.

* * *

As I BLINK my eyes trying to focus, I have an IV in my arm, and I'm lying in a hospital bed. I looked around the room for Genesis, but he isn't in here. The door to the room swings open. I sigh feeling some relief knowing that Genesis is here, but it's Envii.

"Where is Genesis?" I asked.

"He's at a meeting, Envii said and proceeded to drink her Starbucks.

"A meeting? Fuck his meeting call him and get him here right now! Give me your phone I screamed, searching around the room for a phone.

As hot tears started to burn my face, a doctor came into the room. I don't give a fuck about anything he is saying. I need to see Genesis, and that is the only thing that I care about. I screamed at Envii for her phone again, and the doctors asked her did they need to call for back up, and she okayed it. I tried to leap across the rail of the bed to get to her. How the fuck could she tell these people it is okay to fucking restrain me? Why the fuck is she not calling my husband or giving me her phone?

Envii got up and stepped back as the fucking people in the hospital proceeded to restrain me and then she just turned and left out the room. My sister has always had my back. On days when I didn't know what the fuck I was going to do, Envii made a way out of no way for me. The fact that she is just walking away now hurts me in ways I can't even describe. Not only has Genesis turned his back on me, but now so has Envii.

I am starting to get tired of wrestling with these fucking people, so I attempted to calm myself down as much as I can. As more tears started to fall with the thoughts that I have lost my husband all because I just had to go and see Mike one last time. Nothing got resolved, and I didn't tell him anything that I should have.

"Ma'am, are you calm enough that we can let you go now?" a doctor asked, leaning down into my face.

"Yes, I'm fine," I said.

As soon as they all let my arms and legs go, I proceeded to jump on the doctor. No, I'm not fine, and there is nothing that can be done to make me fine. I have nobody left in this world, and the thought of getting high is something that I need right now. Even though this doctor just told me that I overdosed, none of that matters right now because I have nothing else to live for. I bit the doctor in his face causing blood to gush out before the nurses were able to get me off of him. That doesn't matter either. Fuck my life, career, and every damn thing else!

"What the fuck am I paying y'all for? Do y'all muthafucking job! The paperwork has been signed! Y'all got the court order! Do I need to call my fucking attorney?" Envii screamed from outside the doorway as more people came into the room.

GOTTI

*A*s Bron finished cutting my hair, I just keep thinking about hitting the road and getting the fuck out of here for a minute. Truth should be pulling up in a minute so that we can discuss Gionni. The test results came back that Gionni is mine and that saved Giordan her life, but she is cut the fuck off, and I know she never saved anything over the years that Truth or I gave her, so I'm sure that she is back to scamming and selling pussy. I took Gionni from her after I found out that Gionni could possibly be Truth's, and she hasn't seen her since.

Truth has been in Gionni's life longer than I have, and I have enough respect for him as a man to not keep Gionni away from him and his family because she has relationships with his other kids and the rest of his family. We have to be able to communicate for Gionni's sake. Truth is cool. We've been having to communicate for business too, and I haven't had any issue with him so far. Gionni is going with him and his girl, while I go and handle an issue in Arizona.

As I paid Bron, Truth came into the barbershop. Truth and I dapped up as he told me he was late because of shit going on with his baby momma and girl. All I can do is shake my head. I don't have them type of problems in my life, and even though I'm done with Goddess, if a bitch ever tried the shit his bitch is doing, I'd have to fuck her up.

As Truth and I discussed Gionni, my phone started to ring, and it's Envii. The only reason why Envii would be calling me is something that has to do with Goddess, and I don't have shit to say to her. I told her how I felt about going to see Mike and she still took her ass up there to see him. Not only did I almost catch a case for putting my hands on that muthafucka, for her to overdose in the fucking room is just too much drama for me to deal with Goddess. I'm not giving passes, or second chances, and Goddess already knows it should be no surprises when she gets served.

Truth let me know that he would go and get Gionni from school, and she was good for the weekend. I cleared out the barbershop because we need to talk business before I leave. Lady H is sending me to handle some shit that one of her people dropped the ball with, and it's right on time for me. Truth knows the bitch that I am looking for. He used to do business with her until he started fucking her, and that is where the problem started, and now I have to solve it. She suspects Truth to be coming, but I don't know anything about the bitch.

From the pictures that Truth is showing me off his phone, I've never seen her before. Truth is giving me all the information that I need to be able to get to the bitch and everything that I need to know to get the job done. I absorbed all the information and silenced my phone again from Envii's call. I shook up with Truth and made my way out the barbershop.

As soon as my feet hit the concrete, a nigga started shooting in my direction from a black Suburban. I pulled out my heat and started to bust back at the truck while trying to dodge the bullets that are coming as fast as lightning. Truth came out the barbershop busting towards the truck as they skirted off around the corner.

"Gotti, you're hit," Truth said as I scanned my body and saw the blood leaking from my shoulder.

I pulled out my phone and dialed Maci's number. She answered on the second ring and told me she is on the way to my home. I told Truth that I was good, while my arm continued to burn. I took off my coat that is now soaked in my blood and took my shirt off so that I can wrap around the hole in my shoulder. I made my way to my car so that I can make it to the house.

Luckily, it won't take me that long to get home, and the anger that is already in me has just tripled, and some niggas are about to die! I don't know who the fuck could be trying to get at me. We haven't had any problems in the streets. I called E, but he didn't answer. So, I called K, and he answered and let me know that he would meet me at the house.

I pulled up to the house and Maci is already waiting out front. Dr. Maci has come in handy with a lot of situations that have occurred over the years. She is worth every dollar; I hate fucking hospitals. As Maci got her shit together, I'm starting to feel light-headed. I had to lean against the wall to stop myself from falling to the ground. Maci had everything how she wanted to and helped me to sit down. As she started to check my arm, K walked into the room.

"Fuckkkk!" I screamed out as Maci's cold hands touched it.

"Where the fuck is E at?" I asked, trying to get my mind off the pain.

"Nigga, I don't know. I have been looking for him half the damn day. Envii has been getting shit done. I haven't seen the nigga in days. Shit, really since the night he got out," K said.

"There is a piece of the bullet, still in your shoulder, Genesis. This is going to hurt," Maci said.

I tried to prepare myself for the pain that I knew was coming. I have been shot before but this ain't no shit that I can prepare for. I know that I am in good hands with Maci, so I just took the shit as I heard Envii screaming my name from down the hall. I really don't have time to deal with her shit right now. Once she made it the room that we are and she saw what is going on, she shut the fuck up, and K stepped out to talk to her.

"Envii, how long has this bitch been calling you?" K screamed.

"K, watch how the fuck you talking to me. Why the fuck would he be allowing a bitch to call my phone!" Envii screamed.

Maci has been around long enough that she is used to us and how we communicate. As long as she is paid in cash, she has let me know several times that she is blind and deaf to whatever we have going on. I know that it is some shit. I just don't know what. We can't catch a fucking break.

"I got it," Maci said.

I just need her to wrap up my shoulder so that I can see what the fuck is going on. We have been through some shit, and it seems each time shit gets worse. About ten minutes passed and Envii and K, are still going at it, and Maci is bandaging up my shoulder. She finally finished, and I stepped out to go and get her money while K and Envii continued to argue in the hallway.

I grabbed Maci's money and took it to her. She made her way out, and I made my way to find Envii and Kurupt. "So, what the fuck is going on?" I asked, screaming over Envii's loud ass. This bitch is just too damn loud for no fucking reason.

"Somebody's got E and some bitch has been calling her for days telling her that she wanted money to stop fucking Enforcer," K said and then lit a blunt.

"The bitch didn't say anything about her nigga having Enforcer fucking hostage!" Envii spat.

"Who is the bitch, and where is she at?" I asked.

Sitting around talking about what should have been done isn't going to get us anywhere. I need to be able to get on my flight. K called Bri so that she can go and meet the bitch and Envii's phone started ringing. First, some niggas try to take me out, and now some niggas got E. I know it's the same fucking niggas.

"She wants three million, and she not willing to meet me," Envii said.

"I'll send Bri to show her some love," K said, pulling out his phone.

"I got a flight in an hour. Y'all good or do I need to stay here?" I asked.

Kurupt assured me that he has everything under control, so I made my way out. The quicker I get to this bitch in the desert, the quicker I can get back here and get to the niggas that shot at me. I'll handle Giordan when I get back too. Before I could make my way out the door, Envii stopped me talking some shit about Goddess. I shut that shit right the fuck down and made my way out the house.

ENVII

"*I*'ll be back. I'm going to check on Emanii; the nanny just called," I said as I jumped up to make my way out.

I'm fucking lying I wish that bitch would call me right now. I can't keep sitting here waiting for Bri to come back. She has only been out the trap thirty minutes, and I'm losing my fucking mind. Enforcer and I have been going at it for the longest, and it has been sometimes when I said fuck this shit, and he got the fuck out, but the thought of a muthafucking having him doing who knows what to him is not some shit that is sitting well with me. I jumped in my truck and made my way to the hair shop where Bri is supposed to be meeting this bitch Neek at.

I didn't tell anybody but Goddess and Kai about Neek calling me because I figured that E must have been on some of his bullshit that he does and that is why he has been missing. I don't give a fuck if E and I never say another word to each other because I have accepted the part that I played and the secrets that I kept that caused us to fall apart. I pulled up the hair shop, and Bri's car is still out here. What I don't understand is why the fuck it takes so long to drop off some fucking money. What is this bitch doing getting her hair done?

I pulled my truck around to the back door, and I can see that somebody left it cracked open. I popped my truck and opened the secret compartment to get out my Colt AR-15. I don't know who the fuck is in here or what the fuck they got, but I know that I got me. I sent Rocci a text letting her know where I was, and if anything happens, she already knows what to do.

I crept through the back of shop not making any noise, but I can hear niggas and bitches talking. In the back room that leads to the outside is filled with extra hair supplies, a shampoo bowl, and two dryers. Nobody is back here, so I made my way to the front. I checked the room, and I see Brionna doing way too much talking, and I see the duffle bag I gave Bri sitting at this other bitch's feet, so I'm guessing she is Neek. It's one big nigga at the front door blocking it and another nigga sitting on the couch with a blunt hanging out of his mouth talking on the phone.

I came from out the back pushing the door causing it to slam into the wall shooting nonstop at the big nigga until he fell to the ground. Always hit the big nigga first and the rest will sit down. Everybody, but Bri threw their hands up in the air.

"Bitch, cut all this extra talking shit. You've been here for thirty minutes talking," I said, looking at Bri and zipping up my bag of money and kicking it towards her. The least this dumb bitch could do is carry the bag since she couldn't do shit else right. The nigga with the blunt looked scared and confused like he doesn't know what to do. So, I made the choice for him and sent him to where I sent his nigga too.

I understand why K makes some of the decisions he makes, and he is technically the boss of this organization, but I've never been a bitch to play the back and doing what a muthafucka tells me to do is not something that I do easily. As Neek started to cry and scream like somebody was hurting the bitch, I walked up on her to give her something to scream about. I dropped my heat, and my right hand started itching.

A bitch tried to come through the back door, and I pulled out my favorite nine out my pants and sent her to hell. Neek started shaking and crying louder about the girl being her little sister. Some people say their hands itch when they are about to get some money my hand's itch when I'm about to fuck somebody up or kill them. Right now, my hands are on fire. I grabbed Neek by the collar of her shirt with my left hand and beat the fuck out of her with my right.

"I don't give a fuck if the bitch was ya, grandma, if you don't do exactly what the fuck I say and tell me what the fuck I want to know, I'm going to go and see that bitch too," I said, not stopping from fucking her up.

When I felt like she had enough, and both of our shirts were covered in her blood I stopped. I started right away with all my questions. I needed to know who her nigga was and all of his niggas and all they bitches. Every question that I had this bitch answered, and I hit her one more time across her face splitting her nose and made my way out to get my bag to get all the shit I need to tie this bitch up we are about to go for a ride tonight.

I put my AR back into the proper place and threw my money in the trunk. My phone is ringing, and I checked it's K. I'm not answering. I let him run his shit how he sees fit, but I'm not sitting back waiting for him, Gotti, or nobody else to go and get my fucking husband. I'm doing this shit my way and at my fucking speed. I snatched up my shit out my trunk and made my way back in to grab Neek. I put duct tape over her mouth because I'm sick of hearing her fucking mouth, and then I decided to put ass to sleep for a few hours. I was tying her up, and Bri asked me what I wanted her to do.

"I don't want you to do shit for me. Go ask yo boss what he wants you to do!" I spat and proceeded to finish tying Neek up.

I drugged her through the shop and made my way right out to my truck and struggled to get this bitch into the back, but I finally got her in there. I have never needed a bunch of bitches around me to get shit popping. For a long time, it was just Enforcer and me. He and K were friends, but our businesses were separate. The only friend that I have is Rocci, and I trust her with my life because no matter what, she has never switched up on me. I got Goddess and dumb ass Kai now, but neither one of them are out here in the field with me. Rocci is, but I need to handle this shit myself.

Neek's nigga name is Biggz. I've never heard of him, so he can't be somebody too damn important. I pulled up to his right hand's house, Cheese, and his bitch I'm guessing is pulling into the driveway. She has her window rolled down and is screaming at the top of her lungs on the phone with I'm guessing him, asking where he is.

Just the nigga I need to talk to. I slammed my truck in park, jumped out, and made my way around to the driver side of the girl's car. I put my gun in her face in with my right hand and signaled for her to hand me her phone with the left. She handed it right over without saying anything.

"So, this is what I need you to do for me. First of all, shut the fuck up!" I spat as I sent this bitch's head in one direction, and her brains splattered all over the windshield. I pulled her key out the ignition and made my way into their house.

"Everybody that is in here is dead and the longer it takes for Enforcer to be let go, the more bitches, niggas, and their whole damn families that will die in the meantime. So, I need Biggz to call this phone," I said as I unlocked the door.

"Where is my wife? Where is Mo?" Cheese screamed in my ear.

"Dead nigga, and unless you want to join her, that nigga Biggz got five minutes to call me!" I spat and hung up.

I made my way through the house, and it's quiet and still. I don't think anybody is here, but if they are they're going in the trunk with Neek and for the ride too. I have nothing but time, and if this is how these niggas want to play it, then we can play it this way. I went from room to room, and nobody is in this damn house. As I made my way out, I heard something move, and I shot in the direction it was coming from. It was a fucking dog. I'm killing dogs too. Nobody is fucking safe tonight.

As I got into my truck, Mo's phone started to ring, and I answered as I threw the car into drive. Biggz started ranting off his demands and what he wanted in exchange for Enforcer. He wants blocks, traps, and money. He is out of his damn mind along with this bitch in my trunk if the thinks they are getting anything from me but a fucking bullet. I let him finish making his demands.

"You must have me fucked up with some of the punk ass niggas that work for you. I'm not giving you shit, but if you want your wife to make it to her next birthday, you'll listen up to what the fuck you're going to do!" I spat.

I told Biggz that he could meet me in the morning at three in the morning at the Union Station. I made sure that he understands his wife may be breathing and she might be dead depending on how I feel. He agreed, but I'm going to get him tonight. As I hung up on Biggz, K started calling again, and I sent him to the voicemail.

I pulled up two houses down from where Biggz and this bitch in the trunk lay their heads while slamming on the breaks so that this bitch head would smack against the trunk. All his niggas one by one started to make their way out the house until all four of the cars that were in the driveway, but one is gone. I jumped out and made my way around to the trunk. I popped the trunk and pulled the duct tape off of Mo's mouth.

"Who drives a black Denali?" I asked.

"We don't have any black Denalis," Mo said as I hit her in her face just in case she is lying and covered her mouth back up.

I made my way around the back of the house to cut the wires to the alarm system, which wasn't very easy with snow up to my fucking knees. It needs to be done because without the police showing up here. Once the alarm was disabled, I made my way through the first window that I see that isn't locked. I'm in a bedroom, but I can hear two niggas talking outside the door. I leaned up against the door so that I could hear what was being said.

"That nigga fucking my bitch is how I got E, but we gone get the rest of them niggas real soon," a man said.

"What about Envii?" a man asked.

"We are going to get her ass in the morning without a problem before the sun comes up," a man said.

I had heard enough I came out of the room busting, and I have no intentions leaving this house until everybody is dead. I hit one of the niggas in his arm, but he still managed to make it out of the hallway.

The other nigga wasn't so lucky and is on the floor holding his side that is leaking.

"Biggz?" I asked.

"Yea," Biggz managed to say.

"Who was that?" I asked.

"I can't tell—" Biggz said before I killed him.

I entered the code to open up the wall that Neek gave me and entered the code to unlock the volt that Enforcer is in. Since E and I have been together since we were kids, I know that being locked in this volt for five days when he comes out of here he will either be calm and happy to get out or going the fuck off. As I pulled the door open, E got off the ground and came towards me. Normally this would be the time when I would be happy that he is alive, but it's still fuck him. E followed behind me as we made our way back into the office that led to the vault.

We made it outside to my truck, and we got in still not saying anything to each other. What the fuck is it to say? E and I have been having issues for the past two years. I told him that I have a son that I never told him about. I was pregnant when I met him, and then he went to prison shortly after, so by the time he got out, I had already had the baby. My son, Lil' Reek, is being raised by his father Tyreek, and I have been battling back and forth for some time trying to decide if it is the right time to be in my son's life. I was young, and the situation was complicated between his father Tyreek and me.

"Look, Envii, I fucked up," Enforcer said, breaking the silence between us.

I acted like I didn't hear him and kept driving. I just want him the fuck out of my truck, get rid of his bitch, and I can go home. I made mistakes by keeping secrets from Enforcer, but him just thinking that it is acceptable to go around fucking with bitches isn't okay. I don't have to put up with this shit.

Enforcer touched my thigh, and I lost it. I slammed on the breaks and threw the car in park and grabbed my blade out of the center console and started to stab Enforcer. While E was trying to get the knife out of my hand, I started to stab him more. Each time I pulled my blade out of him, I feel a little bit better.

"What the fuck Envii, fucking stop!" Enforcer screamed.

Once I was satisfied and felt that he felt a piece of my pain, I stopped. I have no intentions to kill him because Emanii needs him. My dad was never around, and I always wanted when I had kids to have a family, and that is the reason why I couldn't be there for Lil' Reek. I was a kid, and I never had a real mom, and Tyreek and I could have never been together. As E, screamed out in pain, I got behind the steering wheel to take my husband to the hospital and think about the lie that we are going to tell them when we get there.

GOTTI

As I drive through Tucson, Arizona, Envii is blowing up my damn phone like I owe her money. I'm working and don't have time for her today. The fact that Goddess thought that it was okay to go to see Mike caused shit to be the way that it is between us. I had Iman file paperwork to have power of attorney over Genesis because of addiction so that if anything was to ever happen like what happened the other day, she would have to go into treatment. At the time, Goddess had been clean for a while, and we both agreed that it was for the best.

I wish her the best, and I will make sure that she gets all the treatment that she needs, but I can't be with her anymore. I have to let her go. As much as Envii gets on my damn nerves, she has been there for Goddess from the beginning and will always be.

I'm coming up on the restaurant Blanco Tacos+ Tequila. This is where this bitch I'm looking for goes on Tuesdays. I hope that this is smooth and can get done today so that I can get back home and take care of the muthafuckas that were trying to gun me down. I know that K has shit under control, but I need parts in that shit because they came for me.

I'm looking for a bitch named Regina. She's damn near as black as

112

me but think she's a damn Mexican. That is why she thinks hiding out here is going to save her ass, but she was wrong. The waiter tried to sit me at a table, but I brushed past her and made my way to the bar so that I can see everything that is coming and going in this bitch.

As I ordered my drink, Regina walked in the door. I ordered something to eat because I can't even remember what the last thing that I ate was. Regina sat straight across from me on the other side of the bar. I know that she is going to be here for a while. I can feel her looking at me, but I haven't looked up at her. Envii called again, so I fucking answered so that she can stop calling. I killed my shot, threw some money on the bar and stepped outside so I can talk to her.

"What Envii?" I said as the call connected.

"Why haven't you been to see my sister or called to check on her?" Envii spat.

"I'm handling business, and yo sister is no longer my concern."

"What the fuck do you mean she is no longer yo concern? She is yo fucking wife!" Envii screamed so loud that the Mexican lady walking past me jumped.

"I'm filing for a div—" I attempted to say before I hung up on Envii. Regina was now leaving out of the restaurant.

Envii has her own marriage to be worried about, and mine has never been any of her business, even though she has always thought that it was. It's getting late, so this bitch needs to be heading home so that I can get rid of her and hit the highway.

As I CREPT up Regina stairs, I can hear water running, so she must be in the shower. I hope she enjoyed Taco Tuesday because this will be her last one. After all these years of doing business with Lady H, I still can't believe that people try to cross her and think that they will live long. She doesn't give a fuck about much it seems. Between the stories I've heard, and the shit I have seen with my own eyes, I know that she is not the one to cross and damn sure not over a few dollars. As

Regina sung along to the Lauryn Hill that came from her phone, she didn't even notice me come into the bathroom.

"You had one job to do, and you couldn't do it anyway, so you have to go," I said as I set off several rounds into her body.

As Regina's head smacked the shower making a loud thump and her blood started to make its way down the shower drain, I made my way back out the same way that I came in. My phone started ringing, and I checked to make sure that it wasn't Gionni and it isn't, so I turned it the fuck off. I'll deal with my issues in Colorado when I get back there.

* * *

"MUTHAFUCKA, my sister is pregnant, and you need to get down there to see her right the fuck now!" Envii screamed from across the room in my bedroom.

As I blinked my eyes trying to focus on Envii, I sat up and leaned against my headboard. I know that I heard her right, and I'm not tripping, I just didn't expect to hear any shit like that. This bitch still needs to get the fuck out my house. I didn't respond to Envii, so she is getting mad, and I can feel the heat coming from her from over here.

"I know that you fucking heard me, Gotti. Get the fuck up and go and see my sister!" Envii screamed.

"You can get the fuck out and leave my key downstairs before you leave," I said as I got out my bed and made my way to the bathroom.

I'm not going to lie I'm really surprised to hear that Goddess is pregnant because we tried for a long time to have a baby, and it never happened. We went to specialist tried all types of treatments and still nothing. Goddess was so sick of going back and forth to the doctors and still not getting pregnant that she didn't want to keep going through it.

"Gotti!" Modesty screamed as I stepped out the shower.

I threw on my clothes and made way out to see what the fuck she wants today. She can't ever seem to do the little that I ask of her like take her ass to school, but she doesn't mind asking for something.

With Goddess not being here, she has been losing her mind with not being able to get whatever she wants from her.

"Why the fuck is you screaming? What do you want?" I asked as I came out of my room into the hallway.

"We need to get to the home where Uncle Mike is at. Momma just called. He died," Modesty said.

"Good and I'm not going no damn where," I said as I went back into my room slamming the door.

KURUPT

"**W**here is E at Envii? I need to talk to him about some shit," I asked as Envii made her way into my office.

"In the hospital. He is going to be there for a few days," Envii said, sitting down across me in one of the chairs in front of my desk.

"Envii, what did you do to him?" I asked.

"What needed to be done, but we have a problem. Whoever Biggz is working for is the person that is trying to take us all the fuck out. I went to the mall this morning, and somebody sat my fucking car on fire," Envii said.

"So, are you done doing shit on your own?" I asked.

Envii rolled her eyes and didn't say anything. She was able to get Enforcer and take out a few muthafuckas along the way, but because we don't know who we are dealing with shit could have gone another way. Envii has always done her own thing and getting her to do what is in all of our best interest is always a fucking challenge. I have been trying to find out all night who the fuck is the boss of the niggas, but I haven't found out shit.

If Envii had answered my calls, we could have gotten answers last night, but naw she wanted to do her own thing. After what Envii did last night, none of the niggas showed up to Union station this morning, which isn't surprising. I told Kai that we could go get something to eat, but I got so much shit to take care of. Mina still isn't talking to me and now Alice and me been arguing. I don't have any control over the fact that Krack doesn't want anything to do with her. Now that I know that Krack is fucking with Lady H, I'm not getting involved in that shit.

I need to take Kai out so that we can finally talk and I can explain some shit to her. With all that has been going on, I haven't got the chance to tell her about my new position that Lady H has given me. Truth and I will be taking over working together. I don't know how this is going to go and how her sons are going to take it, but whatever it is, we can take it there. Kai has been really cool and understanding about everything that involves my business, but shit is about to go to another level, and I need to be sure that she understands what this means for all of us.

"Are you ready?" Kai asked, peeking her head into my office.

"Here I come," I said.

I told Envii what I needed her to do, which surprisingly, she didn't give me any attitude and told me she was on it. Gotti has been traveling all over with handling shit all over from Maryland to Vegas that he hasn't been around much. I know that Envii putting Enforcer in the fucking hospital does none of us any good because he could be on the streets getting shit done if she could learn to keep her fucking hands to herself.

Envii and I made our way out of my office. Hope and Kai are making their way down the stairs. Envii ensured me that she would do everything that she needed to do plus Enforcer's part. We are going to see. I know that she has been looking out for Goddess too, but she's gone have to make some shit happen.

We all made our way out the house and to my black Audi A6 and got in. Kai wanted to go to Pappadeaux, so we made our way there. I had to stop at the gas station before I got on the highway. I pulled up to the pump and jumped out to run in and pay for my gas. As I came out, an older mans is up on my car. The gas station is empty other than us. I made my way over to the car and pressed my heat up against the man's back and then turning him around so that I can see his face.

"K, what are you doing? That is just Fat Stevie," Kai said from the car.

I haven't seen Fat Stevie since I was a kid, but a better question is how the fuck does Kai know who he is. We didn't necessarily part on the best of terms. He had me standing on the block all day and night, and I got tired of that shit. He was getting down on me because of my situation with me being out on my own.

Fat Stevie was giving me whatever he wanted, and I was so fucked up at the time that I had no choice but to take it for a minute. I got some shit on consignment from somebody and started selling my own shit that was better than what shit that he was giving me. I took out all his niggas and made it my block. I never gave him what I owed him. After that shit happened, I never saw him again.

"What the fuck do you want Fat Stevie?" I asked.

"What's done is done. I don't want any problems with you. I just wanted to say hi to my daughter," Fat Stevie said, looking at Kai.

"You're what?" Kai asked, rolling down the window further making sure she heard what he said correctly.

I started pumping my gas as Fat Stevie started to tell Kai that he is her biological father, and her mother never wanted her to know. Since he just said that he was getting his shit from Kai then why wait until now to confess this shit. As Fat Stevie continued to talk, tears welled up in Kai's eyes.

I finished pumping the gas and got in the car. All the shit that Fat Stevie is saying about Kai's mom must all be true because of the shit he knows about her from her favorite color to her favorite flower. I hugged Kai as she just continued to cry. I got Fat Stevie's number and let him know that we would be in touch. Nothing is going to get solved in the gas station parking lot. Kai doesn't even talk to her mom, so calling her isn't an option. Kai didn't want to go into the restaurant, so I called from the car to order our food to go. By the time we get there, it should be ready.

Kai didn't say anything, and I didn't either. When Kai is ready to talk, then we will. I don't know what to say about that shit. Alice wasn't shit and stayed on some bullshit, but I knew who my dad was. Even though he wasn't shit either for a long time, we are working on our relationship, so I can't complain now.

We made it to Pappadeaux, and I ran in to get the food. As the man was showing me the food while he packed up the bags, my phone started ringing. I don't know the number, but I answered anyway, and it's E.

"What's up, E?" I said.

"You know that bitch Envii stabbed me the fuck up and I'm in the hospital, right?" E said.

"Then she keeps calling up here asking am I dead yet. I'm sick of her, and all this was because I tried to apologize," E said.

I hear everything that E is saying, but he and Envii have broken up before for a year, and they still found their way back to each other. Envii is extreme and does stay on bullshit, but Enforcer is on always on some good bullshit too.

All our food was right, so I made my way out to the car still on the phone with E. The parking lot only has about five cars in it, but with dinner time coming I'm sure it's about to be packed soon. As soon as I went to grab the door handle, somebody started shooting in my direction. I started shooting back, but there is a nigga in the back seat shooting in at me along with the nigga shooting in the passenger seat.

"Kai, get down!" I screamed as the windshield shattered.

I stopped shooting to get Hope out her seat, but Kai had already grabbed her and put her in the front seat on the ground. I jumped back out the car and started shooting at the niggas again. I hit the nigga in the back seat, and the car skirted out of the parking lot. I jumped in the car so that we can get the fuck out of here. I know somebody done called the police, and I got to get rid of this car. This just made another fucking problem that I don't have time for.

Kai and Hope are okay, so that is all that matters. Hope is still screaming bloody murder, while Kai holds her in the front seat. The way that Kai is looking at me, I know that she wants some fucking answers and that is what I was planning on giving her today, but right now I need to get them home. My phone is shattered, but it still works. I cut my fingers calling Ace and then Big Face so that they can meet me at the house. Mina is at school, but she should be on her way home soon. She is going to be mad, and I can already hear her mouth, but we are going back to around the clock security around this bitch.

* * *

HOPE FINALLY CALMED down and fell asleep, and Mina made it home from school. She came in the house crying her eyes out, so I know something else is wrong. I made my way upstairs to talk to Mina because we are going to have to talk whether she wants to talk or not, shit. I knocked on Mina's bedroom door, and she told me to come in.

"What is wrong, Ahmina?" I asked.

"Tycoon took a deal for seven years," Mina said in between crying.

There is nothing that I can say that is going to make this any easier for Mina and telling her that I tried to warn her isn't going to help either. I grabbed Mina while letting her know that I am going to always be here for her and the baby. There is nothing that I won't do for Mina and these past few months haven't been the easiest, but even with that Mina already knows how hard I go to make sure that we are always good.

After about ten minutes Mina finally stopped crying, so I filled her in on what is going on. Surprisingly, she didn't put up a fight about Big Face and Ace back watching her. Mina and I made our way downstairs, and Bad News and Envii are sitting in the living room. Envii has her gun in her lap.

"Let's talk down the hall," I said.

Shit already was fucked up, but it just got worse. Not only do we still have to take care of the rest of Biggz people before they become a problem, but we also need to find out who the fuck are they working for. Somebody just tried to take me out with my fucking baby and girl in the car. E got this shit started with Biggz and his bitch. I need to get to the hospital and see him. Before Envii could get comfortable in her plush chair, I told her what she needed to do with Bri. I know she doesn't want work with Bri, but this shit needs to get done, and Bri can help her. Envii made her way out the room.

"What did Lady H say?" I asked Bad News.

"She is trying to figure out what is going on herself, but she wanted me to remind you about being at OG's on Sunday," Bad News said.

"So, I found out where Russ and J be at I—" I attempted to say before Kai came into the room.

"K, I need to talk to you," Kai said.

I told her I'd be right out there and finished telling Bad News what I needed him to do. Kai hasn't left the room. She is leaning against the wall waiting for me to finish. After the shit happened earlier, I sat Kai down and told her everything. She kept saying that she wouldn't trust working with Truth, but as long as he stays in his place, we shouldn't have any issues.

GODDESS

"**G**, here this mail was at the house for you," Envii said, handing me the mail as I pushed it out of her hand and onto the ground.

Ever since I was forced to come to this rehab, nothing mattered anymore. I have been here now for forty-five days. Genesis has decided that he is done with me, and I was served this morning with divorce papers. I keep telling Envii to stop coming up here, but every other day, her ass is here. I don't want to be bothered. I just want to be left the fuck alone.

"The only reason why I haven't jumped on you is because we are in here I just want you to know that. Knock something else out of my damn hands, and I'm going to."

Envii picked the mail up off the floor and laid it on the table. Kai walked into the visiting room. I don't want anyone to come and see me. I looked over the mail that Envii brought and seen that most of it is open.

"Why the fuck are you opening my mail?" I asked.

Envii ignored me and spoke to Kai. Kai came around and hugged me and handed me flowers that she brought me. I don't know what the fuck flowers are going to do to help. The fact that I am getting ready to have a child by myself, and to be honest, I'm not sure that I am going to keep it. I haven't said anything to anyone about it, but this is something that I always wanted to share with Genesis and with him deciding to make other plans for his life that won't happen.

Who knows what the fuck is going on at my office? Envii has been there several times, and I can only imagine what the fuck she said to my employees or clients. So, my company will probably be in shambles by the time I am able to get out of here.

"Open that," Envii said, tapping an envelope on the table.

I looked at it, and it is from a law firm. As I opened the envelope, one of the workers came over saying that my daughters were here to see me. I don't have any damn daughters, so I don't know who the fuck could be here to see me.

"I got it," Envii said as she jumped up to go and see who was here.

"I don't want any more visitors," I said as I read over the paperwork.

The documents state that Mike had several insurance policies, and I was the beneficiary for all of them, totaling five million dollars. I can hear my sister screaming from in here. Kai got up to go to try to get her. Everybody in the visiting room is staring at me. I can't go and get her. I can't go past this damn room. I don't give a fuck about Mike or this money. I have written letters and have tried to call Genesis too many times to count, all for him to ignore me. He has the damn number of the facility blocked now.

"That was some of Mike's bitch ass daughters," Envii said as she sat down.

I handed Envii the papers from Mike's lawyers. She started to tell me about what they were saying about wanting money. I don't know why the fuck he left me money, but they can have all that shit. I don't want anything from him or associated with him.

"You're not giving them shit. This money is yours for yo fucking pain and suffering. Fuck him and all those ugly ass kids!" Envii screamed.

I'm not about to argue with Envii about it, but tomorrow when I am able to make professional calls, I am calling Iman so that he can handle it and get the money to whoever. I don't want it, and I'm not about to argue with none of Mike's kids about that money. When Envii told me that Mike died, I didn't feel anything. I was sure that he died after Genesis attacked him, and I collapsed on the floor, but that wasn't the case.

Right now, I have to figure out what I am going to do. That is my only concern. Nothing else matters because when I walk out of here, the only people that I am going to have are Kai and Envii. Envii and Kai caught me up with what was going on with everybody. Even though my life has been flipped upside down, I am happy that things are going well with Kamal and Kai. Kai is happy, and she deserves it and has been through so much.

"I have to go and handle some business. Call me tomorrow," Envii said as she got up to leave.

"So Kai, how are Hope and Mina doing?" I asked.

"They are doing good. Mina and K have been bumping heads, but other than that they're good," Kai said.

"Envii told me about Alice, how is K doing?" I asked.

Genesis walked up on the table before Kai could respond. Kai grabbed up her keys and purse so that she could get out of the building. She came around to hug me, and I still have my eyes on Genesis.

"Why are you here? You want a divorce, remember!" I spat.

As Genesis sat down, I see that he brought his mom here with him. Genesis and Nancy don't have a good relationship. He'll do anything for her financially, or if she needs something done, he will make sure that it gets done, but other than that, they don't really talk. *Why would he bring her here to see me now? Why the fuck did they let them in?*

I don't have a problem with Nancy, but I would rather if I don't talk to you on a regular basis that you do not know anything about my addiction Genesis knows this. Genesis hasn't said anything, but we are still having a stare off. Nancy is still looking around and hasn't said anything either.

"Why did you come here, Genesis?" I asked.

Nancy finally sat down and reached across the table for my hand. Genesis and I have had our issues over the years, but the way that he is handling this situation, I would have never imagined this. I feel like he is treating me like he treats people in the streets. When I got with Genesis, I told him everything there was to know about me. Things that I would never tell anybody else. He understands me in a way that no one else ever has, but when I look at him now, the love that used to be in his eyes when he saw me is not there anymore.

"The private room is ready for you now, Mr. Braxton," Amanda one of the workers said.

"Thank you," Genesis said, standing up.

I'm relieved that Genesis got the private room. I would like to know why Nancy is here. The conversation that Genesis and I need to have, I would rather not have it in front of her. We made our way into the room, and Genesis' phone started ringing, and he jumped up and made his way out of the room. I know the life that Genesis lives, and I know what comes with it. It has never come before me, and he has always turned off the streets when I was in his presence.

Seeing him walk out of the door because of his phone is ringing is just affirmation that we are really over, and there is nothing that I can say or do that will get things back to how they were.

"I have a question Goddess, what was your relationship with Mike ?" Nancy asked.

"You already know the answer to that I'm sure considering the fact that he was your brother or your late husband's brother," I said, folding my arms over my chest.

"Mike was my brother, and my husband isn't dead. Is that what Genesis told you?" Nancy asked.

"What do you mean he isn't dead?" I asked.

First Genesis doesn't tell me that Mike is his uncle, and then he also lied about the fact that his father was dead. Who the fuck lies about that? As hard as it was, I told Genesis everything about my family. Even the shit with Leonard that I have never told anybody. As Genesis came back into the room, I stopped listening to Nancy and everything she is saying.

"Why wouldn't you tell me that Mike was your uncle? And why have you been lying to me telling me that your dad is dead?" I asked.

"Who gives a fuck about Mike being my uncle and my dad is dead. The nigga is dead to me!" Genesis screamed.

Nancy tried to get Genesis to calm down and sit down, but he's mad as hell that she told me about his dad, and he isn't listening to anything that she has said. The rage that is in Genesis' eyes I have never seen before. Very few times has he ever raised his voice, let alone raised his hand to me, but now I don't know what to expect from him.

"Kill, my baby, and I'll kill you," Genesis said, leaning over the table into my face.

How the fuck does he know that I had scheduled an abortion. This shit is supposed to be confidential. Genesis made his way out of the room and slammed the door behind him. As Nancy tried to explain to me about Genesis father, a lot of things started to make sense. When Genesis and I were planning to get married, he refused to go to a church but would not tell me why. Then she went on to tell me that Genesis told her when he was a kid that Mike had been touching him and she didn't believe him until recently when other relatives started to say that he did shit to them too. As tears ran down my face I wanted to get up and go after Genesis, but I can't leave the building, and I know that he is long gone.

Nancy got up from her seat and wrapped her arms around me, but the only thing that did was make me cry harder than I already am. All I want is Genesis to understand that I messed up, and I want to make things right between us. Talking to Nancy about any of Genesis and my problems would be a waste of time. He barely answers her calls, so taking advice from her is out of the question.

KURUPT

*A*s we sit in the front row of this fucking church, all I want to do is get the fuck out of here. Kai has been here every step of the way, but it's nothing that she or nobody else can do to bring Alice back. Mina is laying her head on my arm as she continues to cry. I agreed to this funeral for Re-Re, but if they don't speed this bitch up, I'm going to be leaving real fucking soon.

Somebody killed my mom a three days ago in her house. What fucks me up the most is that she just got back in our lives. The fact that I don't have any idea of who the fuck did this to my momma is making this shit even harder, but the way that it was done, it had to be some shit to get back at me. Hope is sleep in Kai's arms, and all I want to do is get in the streets and see what the fuck I can find out.

Ever since whoever shot up my car, shot at Gotti, and set Envii's car on fire, we haven't had any issues. We have killed everybody working for Biggz but haven't got anywhere with finding out who the fuck they were working for. Since I started working with Truth, he has been trying to find out any information but hasn't come back with anything either.

Until they came for Alice, I was willing to just play it cool for a while like I have been doing, but now it's over. Kai's birthday is this weekend, and we have plans to go to Vegas. She keeps saying that we don't have to go, but I'm not going to cancel her birthday trip. She has been here for Mina, Hope, and I a lot, and she deserves it.

Mina, Kai, and I made our way up to the casket before they closed it. I felt somebody tap me on the shoulder, and I turned around, and it's my dad. I didn't know if he was going to be able to make it here since he left town just a few days ago.

I looked around the church to see if I see some muthafuckas that shouldn't be here. As soon as I turned around, niggas that I thought were the funeral home workers started busting in our direction. I got Kai, Mina, and Hope on the ground and reached into Alice's casket to get my AR-15 while busting with my Glock that was on my waist. I looked over at Krack, and he was busting with me. Gotti will not come into a church, so he isn't here, and that nigga Enforcer is still fucking cripple.

"Do not get up until I come and get y'all," I said as I made my way closer to get the rest of these niggas.

It started off being fifteen of these niggas, and now it's still eight standing the number of people that they got against Krack and me. All the rounds that they are shooting are just tearing up bibles and riddling the pews. I ducked behind a pew trying to dodge some of the bullets that are coming in my direction and looked over the pew to see Rocci and Envii coming in the church Envii has an air rifle and is letting it go with each step that she makes to come further in the church. Rocci is shooting just as many bullets as she made her way inside. They were not expecting anybody to come from the back and shit neither was I.

I ran back up to the front to get my family the fuck out of here and home. Envii let me know that she would make sure that Alice made it to the cemetery. I called Treach multiple times to see how the fuck did these muthafuckas that I thought work for him get the fuck in. When I came to their funeral home about burying Alice, he insured me and gave me peace of mind he would make everything smooth and all this bullshit while continuing to call me bra. The last thing that I need right now is another sibling, and I don't give a fuck that Krack is supposed to be his dad.

As soon as I make sure that my family is home and good, I'm going to see that nigga. Hope is still screaming, and Kai is in the back seat with her. I think between Tycoon getting sent away and then momma dying that Mina is all cried out. Lately, her attitude and whole demeanor have changed. We pulled up to the house, and Gotti, Bad News, Ace and Big Face are all in the driveway.

Hope finally stopped screaming, and I kissed her on the forehead before I ran upstairs to grab some shit. I can tell by the look on Kai's face that she is worried about what is going to happen next. I don't know how she is going to take what I am about to tell her, but right now this is what is best for us. I have to make sure that we will always be good and allowing this shit to linger on with whoever is coming for us can't continue.

I came out of my closet and Kai is standing in our bedroom door-way. I can tell that she wants answers, and she doesn't want me to leave right now, but I have to. I turned on the shower and walked back into the bedroom.

"Kai, I have to leave for a while until I can handle this shit," I said as I walked up on Kai pulling her closer to me and embracing her.

Kai didn't say anything, but her tears started to wet up my shirt. I hope that I don't have to be gone too long away from her, Hope, and Mina, but I have to handle this shit now so that we can go on with our lives. Kai pulled away from a little and looked up at me.

"Alright, I understand this is what you have to do."

I kissed Kai and held on to her tighter I am going to do what I have to do to make sure that I make it back to her in one piece. Kai and I made our way downstairs, and Mina is standing at the bottom of the stairs. She is getting big as hell, and she is having a little girl. Mina keeps saying that she is waiting for Tycoon to come home, but I know that isn't going to last long.

"Ahmina, let me talk to you for a second," I said and hugged Kai, and she made her way down the hall.

"Yea," Mina said.

"I have to go and take care of some shit. I don't know how long I'm going to be gone, but I'm coming back. Ace is going to be here with y'all," I said.

"Okay. Are you going to find out who killed momma?" Mina asked while hugging me.

"I'm going to handle that, Mina."

* * *

"I'M NOT LEAVING this muthafucka until you find out who the fuck was behind this. I came to you to bury my momma, and you gave me yo word, and that shit didn't go down like it was supposed to. My momma's casket is riddled with fucking bullets. The niggas that we laid down were dressed like yo people and were seating people. If you don't know who the fuck they were, then somebody in this bitch does. How the fuck they have the same uniforms as yo people? Nigga, you gone tell me something!" I spat.

I have lost all patience, and if we have to spend the night in this damn funeral home that is what it will be because I'm not leaving until I know something. This nigga knows just as much about the streets as I do. His momma is Lady Heroin.

"Let me see, what I can find out," Treach said, adjusting his tie.

Gotti is standing by the door. I nodded my head saying that it was okay to let him out of his office. I know that he feels real disrespected and uncomfortable about how me and my people have just ambushed his office, but I don't give a fuck. Envii and Rocci are in the parking lot, and I have a nigga by every door. Nobody will be coming in or out of this bitch unless I give the word. Nobody ain't going home, including the damn secretaries, until I find out what I need to know.

"Why the fuck is Rocci with Envii?" I asked.

"I don't know, nigga. I was wondering the same shit!" Gotti spat, lighting a blunt.

My phone started ringing, and it's Krack. I answered, and he wanted to know did I need anything. I told him that I have everything under control. He told me that he would see what he could find out and be in touch. This is some personal shit, so whatever business that Truth and I have don't have shit to do with this unless he can point me in the direction of the muthafucka that has been in on this shit. I have talked to Truth several times, and he says that he doesn't have any information. I know that if Lady H knew anything, she would have sent word, but she hasn't.

"Okay, look, K. It looks like one of our employees took the uniforms. That's Mazi," Tyreek said, showing me the video recording on an iPad.

I don't give a fuck who took the fucking uniforms. I need to know who they are, where they live, and the same information about everything breathing that is close to them. I'm just watching this muthafucka Tyreek as he keeps rewinding this damn video, showing me the same nigga taking uniforms.

"Clearly, I haven't made myself clear on what the fuck I need from you," I said, snatching the iPad out of his hand and throwing it into the wall, causing it to crack into hundreds of pieces that are flying in every direction.

As I gave Tyreek specific detailed instructions on what the fuck I wanted, he backed up and just looked at me. I got up from the chair that I am sitting in and made my way around his desk and sat in his chair. Maybe this will send the message that seems to be going over his fucking head. He supposed to be so damn smart, but I can't tell. I can tell by the look on his face that he wants me to get the fuck out, but I 'm not going anywhere. He damned near stomped out like a bitch as his shoes taped across the room to the door and down the hallway.

"Nigga that's Mina's big sister, not brother," Gotti said, laughing. That's how the fuck I'm feeling right about now. I mean damn, what the fuck? Is this that damn hard?

"Aye, Big Face go get that secretary and bring her here," I said.

Let's see if I can get my brother some help because clearly, he needs somebody to hold his hand and help him. Big face left out the room. I can tell by the look on Gotti's face that his head is somewhere else with all that is going on between him and Goddess, but he hasn't said anything about what they are going through. I only know what I know because of Kai.

Gotti has been in the streets nonstop ever since Goddess went to rehab. He is doing anything and everything just to stay busy. Big Face brought the secretary into the office. I whispered in Bad News' ear to tell him what I needed to be done, and he left out the room. This lady's pale face is as red as a stop sign, and the way she is shaking like she is terrified.

"Do you handle payroll?" I asked.

"Yes...yes, sir," the lady responded.

"Alright pull up Mazi's information," I said, scooting back so that she can get to the computer.

Tyreek made his way into the office, and the secretary made her way around the desk and is logging onto to the computer. Tyreek handed me a file, I looked through it, and it is all Mazi's info.

"Gotti, I'll be right back," I said as I stood up and made my way out to check out this information. Nobody is leaving here until I know that this shit is accurate, and Mazi answers a few questions for me about who he works for.

GOTTI

If this nigga Tyreek huff and puff one more muthafucking time, I'm going to silence his ass forever. He ain't my damn long-lost brother, and he is getting on my damn nerves. I can think of other shit that I could be doing with my Friday night, but due to him not handling his business, we are here. It's something about this nigga that I do not like, and I told K that shit.

The fact that his baby momma is sitting in the parking lot isn't making it any better. He keeps stepping out of his office to take phone calls. It's damn near one o' clock in the morning, and he doesn't handle shit in the streets, so I would like to know who planning a funeral this time of night.

My phone started ringing, and it's Goddess. This is the first time she has tried to call since I left the rehab center. I unblocked her when I left, but I haven't been back up there, and that was a week ago. The shit that my momma told her was some shit that wasn't any of Goddesses fucking business. I haven't talked to her either since she told me that she told Goddess that shit. The shit that Mike did to me is something that has haunted me ever since that shit happened.

It's not something that I think about all the time, but it's some shit that I think about every now and again. It is something that I will never forget when he used to come into my room. I hear some fucking yelling and screaming outside the door, so I jumped up off the couch and made my way out to see what the fuck is going on.

"Nigga, you're not going nowhere until we get what we need. So. unless you have some more information that can speed this the fuck up, I suggest you sit the fuck down and relax!" I spat as Bad News stood in front of the door, preventing Tyreek from getting out.

This nigga still standing in front of Bad New like he is about to blow Bad News out of his way and make it outside. I made my way across the room and pulled out my Berretta and walked around so that I could look Tyreek in the eyes. That hate and resentment that he has that he ain't us is dancing in his eyes like it has from the first day we met him. I took my gun and smacked it across Tyreek's face and continued to over and over until that nigga fell to the ground and his blood splattered all over my shirt. I got enough shit going on than to be repeating myself to grown muthafuckas.

* * *

"Mazi said that he is working for his cousin, but he's not telling me his name!" K spat.

"Where the fuck is he at?" I asked.

"In my trunk!" K spat.

"While you were gone, I was able to get information about Mazi's cousin Kurt," Tyreek said.

We have been here for hours, and this nigga ain't said shit to me, but he found out new information. The sun is coming up, and we could have possibly been the fuck out of here, but he waits until now after I done already had to fuck him up. If it weren't for K, I would have killed this nigga. I made my way outside, and Envii and Rocci are still sitting in the car. After taking a few hits from my blunt, I made my way back inside the funeral home.

K is talking to Tyreek, but I can tell that he has lost all patience with dealing with this goofy nigga.

"If I go and check this nigga out and it's not what you are telling me, then I'm going to kill you," K said as he got up and told me to roll with him. If I don't then he would have come back to a dead brother because how dumb can this nigga be?

As K and I rode to see this nigga Kurt, my mom started calling. I'll go and see her after I handle this, but not right now I can't talk to her. She decided that she wanted to get help and has been doing good as far as I know, but to be real, I don't have any expectations for her staying clean because the hope that I had has all gone away.

We finally made it to where Kurt is supposed to be and jumped out the car. I have never heard of this nigga Kurt, so why he would be gunning for us, I don't know, but we are about to find out. Once we let ourselves in the house, I can hear some noise coming from upstairs, so we made our way up there. K is leading the way, and I'm checking all the rooms as we made our way down the hall. They are all empty, and K is getting madder with each room that is empty. The last one where the TV is blasting isn't empty. K hit the nigga in the bed in the stomach and woke him up.

"You been looking for me?" K asked, leaning against the dresser.

"Yea!" the Kurt nigga spat.

As he told us he was told to take out all of us in exchange for a seat at a very powerful table, K and I both started laughing. I'm curious who the fuck could have offered him that. This nigga doesn't have a care in the world. He knows what is about to happen before we leave out of here.

"Who sent you?" K asked.

"G," Kurt said.

"Who the fuck is G?" K asked.

"Giordan."

K turned to look at me as I filled Kurt with bullets. Ain't this a bitch. Now the bitch is trying to get me killed. I need to get the fuck out of here and go and find this bitch immediately. She was never a threat, so with all this other shit going on, I hadn't made it to her yet.

As I stormed out the room and down the hall, I can hear K's footsteps behind me. I have never done anything to this bitch Giordan. The only thing I have done is kept money in her pockets and made sure that she was good. She fucked up whatever we had a long time ago. I wasn't willing to fuck her, but I'm sure the bitch ain't been dick deprived in all these years. As K and I rode back to the funeral home neither one of said anything to each other. With the shit that I need to do, there isn't going to much talking involved. We pulled back up to the funeral home, and K told me to go and handle my business he had everything else under control.

I made my way to see Giordan as Modesty name popped up on my dashboard. I can't talk to her right now, and then Gionni's name popped up right after, but I'll call as soon as I'm done. I got to Giordan's, and I see her car in the driveway, so I pulled around to the back. I jumped out and let myself in the back door.

I can hear music playing upstairs, so I made my way up there. I went to her room, but she isn't in there. I pushed open each door, and she isn't in any of them. As I pushed open the door to the bathroom, she damn near jumped out of the tub. I grabbed her by her hair, knocking over candles that are burning in the process.

Once we got into the hallway, I pulled out my heat and put it to her head.

"Wait, wait, wait. Please no, I'm sorry I didn't want to do it, but somebody made me. Treach told me if I didn't do it, they would kill Gionni and me," Giordan whined.

I know this bitch is lying, so I just acted like I didn't hear anything she said and sent her ass to hell. I'll see her when I get there. If any of that shit was the truth, then why the fuck wouldn't she had said something way before now while she is sitting over here in la la fucking land.

I made my way out while calling the clean-up crew to take care of this place if the candles don't burn this bitch to the ground first. At this point, either way is fine by me. I called K to let him know that it was her ass and made my way to change my clothes and check on Gionni and Modesty.

KAI MORAE

"*K*ai, get up. Yellow, get up," K said.

I turned over and acted like I didn't hear him. This is the first in months that I have been able to sleep in, and I'm not getting up. Things have finally got to where we don't have a new problem every other day. Two months ago, that week that K was gone was one of the hardest weeks ever. I didn't know what the fuck was going on or if he was okay. I can't complain about anything now. Mina and I both just finished another semester of school, and we both made the dean's list, and K hasn't had to be gone for long or very often here lately.

"Kai, get up!" K yelled again.

"What Kamal? I'm tired," I whined as I turned around to face him.

Blinking my eyes to focus on K, he is fully dressed and has Hope in his arms. I grabbed my phone to see what time it is. It's not even eight in the morning.

"Get up and get dressed. We got to be at the airport in two hours," K said, slapping my ass and turning to walk away.

"Where are we going?" I asked.

"You'll see when we get there," K said before he disappeared out the room.

I jumped up to get in the shower and got myself together so that we can leave. We haven't been anywhere in a while, so I'm happy to be leaving since I have a break before the next semester starts. I haven't been in the shower a good five minutes, and K is already calling my name. I jumped out the shower, dried off, and put lotion all over my body, brushed my teeth, and walked into my closet still ignoring K screaming my name.

I don't know where we are going so, I grabbed a burgundy Nike jogging suit to wear to the airport and put it on. I looked over at my shoes to see which tennis shoes I'm going to put on, and K is standing in the doorway.

"I love you, Kai," K said.

"I love you too."

"Hurry yo ass up before I leave you and go by myself," K said and walked away.

He still is going to have to wait because I still need to pack. Mina came into the closet. "Put on these shoes and go, Kai." *Why the hell is she trying to rush us out of the house?*

Mina started, pulling my arm saying that K isn't taking any bags either. She doesn't give a damn about K being ready to go. She is trying to get rid of me. She is so big and next weekend is her baby shower, so I know that we'll be back at least by then. I yanked away from Mina and went to get my hair together.

I have a sew-in, so I just ran the flat iron over my edges, and I'm good. I made my way downstairs, so K can quit screaming my name. He still has Hope in his arms, so he isn't too ready to go, I took Hope from him, and before I could kiss and hug her, Mina had snatched her from me. K pulled me by my arm and out the house.

* * *

K and I walked into the Palazzo in Las Vegas, and it's beautiful. I didn't know where we were going until we landed, and I saw the sign. This is to make up for not being able to do what we planned for my birthday. He has been on and off the phone since we got off the plane

138

but took my phone and won't give it back. We made our way through the hotel and to the elevator to get up to the chairman suite. I want to go and see Vegas, but honestly, I just want to take a nap. I'm so damn tired. I know that K is trying to get downstairs to gamble.

We made it to our suite, and this is beautiful. This suite is big as hell and has three bedrooms, two living rooms, three bathrooms, a dining room, and patio. I made my way right to the master bedroom so that I can take a nap. I know K is about to be talking shit, but I just need a few hours. I turned the TV on and signed into Pandora.

"Ut-unn get the hell up. We need to go and get clothes and shit. Why are you so tired? You pregnant?" K asked.

"No, K. I'm tired. Let me just sleep for a few hours and then we can go," I whined.

"Nope," K said, pulling the covers off me and closer to him.

As Raphael Saadiq "Ask of You" played in the background, K pulled my pants off. K slipped off his J's and made his way on the bed, kissing my box through my panties. I am trying to prepare myself for his mouth. Got damn his mouth; it gets better and better every time. My pussy is already drenched, and K knows just what to do to make it wetter.

K took off my panties and took both of my thighs into his embrace and dove into my honey pot. The way that K is flicking his tongue has me reaching for shit to grab. K is gripping my thighs tight, and the chances of me getting away if I wanted to is slim. As K picked up the speed and loosened his grip on my thighs, I started to grind on his tongue. As I came, K kept on going and doing his muthafucking thang.

After a few more minutes I came again, and K ate it all up and came out of his clothes. Even though I sleep next to K every night, the sight of my man's body is something. I get excited to see every time I see it. His body is so right, and you can tell that the hours he spends in our gym have paid off. His dick makes my mouth water at the sight of it. It's just so damn perfect. As K made his way into me, we both gasped like it was the first time. Each stroke that K gives just make me want more and more. K picked up the speed threw my legs over his shoulders and began to hit places that I didn't know existed.

"Ooooh, shit K, Right there!" I finally said.

That had been stuck in my throat since he started. Saying that was like putting a battery in K's back and just made him go even harder while I was screaming out his name and he was making me more of his than I already am. K and I came, and he laid on me while still inside of me. I'm trying to catch my breath, and he got up and pulled me into the bathroom for some more.

* * *

"You sleepy?" K asked as we walked the strip holding hands.

"Yea," I said in between yawning.

"One more place, and then we'll go back to the room."

We have been here for three days, and we go home in the morning. As we walk, I keep seeing these signs about a helicopter ride. I hope he doesn't think we about to get on a damn helicopter. I don't really like planes, let alone no small ass helicopter. As we got up to a bigger sign with an arrow pointing that clearly says *helicopter rides*, I stopped in my tracks, which causes K to stop.

"Bring yo scary ass on; I got you," K said, pulling me into the building.

The lady at the front desk handed us our headphones, and then we made our way to the helicopter. As the pilot gave us all the instructions, all I kept thinking about is we better make it back here in one piece, while K thinks it's so funny that I'm scared.

It's not as bad as I thought it would be, so I'm good. I stopped looking out the window and looked over, and Kamal is staring at me. The pilot announced what we are coming up on as K and I both looked to see the Grand Canyon.

"Kai, you know that I love you, right?" K asked me to take my attention away from sightseeing.

"Yea, I love you too," I said, looking over at him he has a jewelry box in his hand.

"What's that?" I asked.

"We done been through some shit, and we have had our ups and downs, but I know that you are the woman that I want to wake up to every morning. Even when you get on my damn nerves, I still wouldn't want to be with nobody else," K said as tears started to fall from my eyes and I swung on him for that last part. I don't be getting on his nerves. He be getting on mine. K wiped my tears away.

"I want this forever, Yellow. Will you marry me?" K asked.

Tears continue to fall, and my answer was stuck in my throat. I couldn't it get out as I nodded my head and hugged K tight never wanting to let him go. In a short amount of time K has come into my life and made everything that was wrong right. K loves all my imperfections, and which is one of the reasons why I want this forever and a day. Even though I know that this is happening, it still doesn't seem real.

KURUPT

"Kai, hurry up this lady down here!" I screamed up the stairs.

It's been three months since I proposed and today is our engagement party. Envii and Rocci made their way through the front door. I made my way back to the theater with Gotti and E. Everything has been good these past few months. I can't complain as long as my people are good and happy, then I'm happy. Mina had the baby, and she stopped talking about moving out which is fine by me. I wish she would move on with her life and quit talking to Tycoon, but I'm not going to get into that with her.

"Why the fuck does Envii keep bringing Rocci around?" I asked as I sat down.

"Shit, I was about to ask the same thing," Gotti said.

The party is starting in a few hours, and my house is full of decorators, chefs, waiters, and a whole bunch of other muthafuckas that I want out my house.

"E, Emanii is here I'm out," Envii said from behind me.

I turned around, and Rocci is standing in the doorway. The way she is looking at me she is saying come play with my pussy. I turned my ass right back around and got back to the game. Envii made her way out the room, and I'm just ready for this shit to start so that it can be over with. I hope that Envii doesn't jump on Katrina today because I know that she is coming if she isn't already here.

I jumped up to go and remind Envii that it won't be any of that shit in my house just in case she forgot. As I got to the front to catch Envii before she leaves, Yellow is coming down the stairs. Kai is so beautiful, and I love everything about her ass. She is the only reason why I'm willing to put up with all these damn parties.

"Envii, don't start no shit in my house later," I said.

Envii didn't answer; she walked out. But, if her ass jumps bad, she'll be getting put out just like anybody else. I'm not about to play with Envii. I'm not E, and she is not about to fuck up today on her bullshit. Kai is pulling my shirt telling me to go and get dressed before people start showing up. As the party planner pulled her away, I made my way upstairs to get dressed. I looked in Hope's room to check on her, and she's sleep, but I see Kai already got her dressed and combed her hair.

"K!" Mina screamed from down the hall.

"Yea, Mina," I said as I came up on her room.

"Will you or Kai watch Ta'Shell for me tonight?"

"Where are you going?"

"On a date," Mina said which surprised me.

I walked away without answering, but she already knows I'm not going to say no. I just hope that it's a man and not another fucking Tycoon. Shit, that was music to my ears hearing that. If she is going on dates, that means that she is done going up to Sterling to see Tycoon. I don't like that shit and never did. I just would have Ace driving her back and forth.

THIS PARTY IS ALMOST OVER, I checked myself in the mirror and made my way out the bathroom as I was met by Rocci, standing outside my damn bedroom door. "How can I fucking help you?" I asked, brushing her hands off me. I haven't fucked with Rocci in years, and her suddenly popping back up I knew there had to be some bullshit behind it. We used to fuck with each other a few years back, but it didn't work out. Well, I was sick of her, and she talked too damn much, and I couldn't take it. Not to mention she was trying to be Bonnie, and that ain't my thing. I don't want any female in the field with me, and she couldn't understand that.

"I know you miss me," Rocci said, trying to touch my dick.

"Naw, I'm good on you, and you already know that. I'm trying to figure out why are you here?" I spat, pushing Rocci's hands off me.

"I miss you, and I want things to go back to how they used to be," Rocci said with her words slurring.

I walked away from her drunk ass because she must be out of her mind. As she picked up her pace trying to get to me, I made my way downstairs to find Envii to get this bitch out my house before I have Ace kick her ass out. There was no bad blood between Rocci and me, but I'm not interested, and to try this shit right now at my damn engagement party is out of line. I don't even know why the fuck she came. As I got to the bottom of the stairs, Envii walked up.

"Get this bitch out my house and don't ever bring her ass back!" I spat. I made my way back into the living room where everybody is.

Kai is so happy, smiling and shit. When I met her, she never used to smile, and I'm going to make sure that I do whatever it takes to make sure that she is happy forever.

Goddess is here, but she isn't here with Gotti. Envii is here, but she ain't here with E. It seems like all my niggas and they girls are falling off. Envii and E, I'm not surprised about what's going on with them, but Goddess and Gotti, I never would have thought that would happen to them. Goddess finished rehab and came home, and Gotti moved out.

"I just want to make a toast to my nigga K and Kai," Gotti screamed over a microphone.

Hope came up pulling my pants leg as everybody threw their glasses in the air. I picked her up as everybody clinked their glasses together. Goddess and Kai left out the room after the toast. I can hear Envii cussing out Rocci over the music at the front door. They can do that shit outside. E nodded his head at me as he made his way in that direction.

Hope wanted some cake, so I went into the other room where the cake is to get her some as I walked in I can hear Kai and Goddess talking.

"I just saw, her trying to touch on K," Kai said. Goddess insured her that I'm not interested in Rocci.

I can tell from Kai's tone that she has an attitude, and I know she can fucking hear Envii screaming like the other thirty people here. I got Hope her cake and made my way out the room. Here we go with some bullshit.

* * *

As I turned over Kai, isn't in bed. I got up and made my way downstairs to the room she is always in reading and doing her homework. I know that is where she probably is. As I came down the stairs, E and Katrina are going up the stairs. I want this nigga out of my house and tomorrow is the day he has to go. Kai is on the phone as I walked into the room the phone is on speaker, and it's her Aunt Audrey. None of them came to our engagement party except Audrey. Kai kept saying she was good and it didn't matter, but I know that is not the case.

They still haven't really been fucking with her since Deontae killed her cousin. We never really talk about it, but I can tell that shit is fucking with her around the holidays. They don't call or nothing but fuck them! We got each other, and I tell her that every day. I want to tell Kai about Rocci, but she hasn't said anything, so I'm not going to bring it up. She doesn't have an attitude or nothing anymore, so Goddess must have eased her mind. I grabbed Kai's hand and told auntie bye, and Yellow got up and led the way back to our bedroom.

ENVII

"To be honest with you, Tuesday, I don't give not one fuck about what is going on in yo personal life, I'm ya boss! You think if you go to Santander and tell them about ya baby daddy and his new bitch, they are going to let you miss work? Bitch, they're not, and neither am I! Get yo ass back to the spot, or yo ass will be going to apply for TANIF!" I screamed into the phone and hung up on her ass.

I have been sitting in front of Kurupt's thinking of a million excuses for over an hour about why I don't need to go in here. E and I have been through some shit over the past few years, and I thought that me beating up bitches, causing scenes, killing hoes, and that shit would change, but it hasn't. I'm sick of this shit. Yea, I've made some mistakes, but I can't keep allowing E to do me like he has been. Time and time again I take his ass back, and nothing really changes.

My daughter is old enough to know that something isn't right, and I can't keep letting her see me be like this all because E wants to go around fucking this bitch and that bitch. It took everything in me not to shoot Katrina at Kai's and Kurupt's engagement party, but what the fuck is that going to change? In another week it will be another

Katrina. I put out my blunt, got out the car, and made my way into K's. Kai told me that E is doing his physical therapy, so his ass is here for sure. Kai came to the door and let me in.

"Hey Envii, I'm running late. I'll talk to you later," Kai said, running past me.

I made my way to the gym, and each step that I take gets harder and harder. I always wanted E and me to work. I walked away from somebody else just so we can be together. Every day lately, I've been thinking that I made a mistake. E and I have always had problems, but the disrespect with bitches came after I told him about my son. I should have told him from the beginning, but I didn't because it killed me every day that I wasn't in his life. I am still going back and forth with Tyreek about talking to my son.

As I walked in the gym, this little blonde hair blued eyes bitch with no ass is packing up her shit. E looked over and seen me. He smiled at me, but I can't return it. E has broken me down on the inside to a place that I never would allow anyone else to. E thinks because we have so much history that no matter what I'll always be down.

"This is my wife, Ericka," E said.

"Hi, nice to meet you. I've heard a lot about you," Becky with the good hair said, extending her hand.

I looked her up and down and walked over to E who is shaking his head. I'm not interested in getting to know her ass, and E knew that shit when he attempted to introduce us. He is probably fucking her too. E stood up from the weight bench and tried to grab my hand and pulled away.

"My dad and 'em want to see Emanii," E said.

I heard him, but I don't give a damn about them seeing Emanii. They don't like me, and I don't like them, not to mention I don't fucking trust them. E already knows how I feel about his dad and stepmom, so he can miss me with that.

"You know I have been fucked up thinking about that shit that happened. I don't know why now, but that shit been popping into my head a lot lately," E said.

I know what he is talking about, but I don't want to think about that, and that is some shit that I am dealing with myself. E and I met when we were both locked up in substance abuse and mental health treatment center. I was fourteen, and he was seventeen at the time, and even though it was a while back, the shit that we went through there being locked in the box for days being let out for an hour still has me fucked up here and there. E dealt with it for longer than I did because when he turned eighteen, they came and picked him up and took him to prison for two more years on top of the two he had already had done.

"Look, I can't do this no more. You can have somebody come and get yo shit, or I can bring it here, but I'm done," I said, throwing the divorce papers that I just got from Iman in his face.

As I stormed out of the room, hot tears burned my face, and I just let them fall. As I walked down the hallway, I can hear Enforcer screaming my name. He can't walk that fast with his cripple ass, so he can't come after me. I bumped into K on my way down the hall, but I didn't say anything, and neither did he. I can feel a weight lifting off my shoulders with each step that I take.

"Envii!" Mina screamed.

I can't talk to her right now, I'm a fucking mess, and all I want to do is go home and get in my bed. Goddess is getting Emanii from school, and I don't plan on leaving my house unless I have to, or unless I burn that muthafucka to the ground and walk away from that too. My phone started ringing, and I looked down at it as I got in the car. It's Rocci. I don't have shit to say to her. She was on some good bullshit trying to get with K at his fucking engagement party while her broke ass baby daddy is at home laying on her couch playing video games.

It's some shit that you just don't do, and she knows she was dead ass wrong. She hasn't said shit about K in years. So, the shit caught me off guard. I know that Rocci isn't in the best situation because she feels stuck with her baby daddy, but K isn't going to be the nigga to save her, so I suggested that she keep looking for him. I haven't talked to her since that night. I'll call her ass later. I have my own problems to deal with today. As I drove down the highway, my phone started ringing again, and it's E. I threw that muthafucka across three lanes and kept going.

GODDESS

$\mathcal{A}$s I lay on the cold table, I never imagined that I would be doing this alone. Genesis is still barely talking to me. He won't stay at the house, and when I offered to leave, he went the fuck off. We only talk when we absolutely have to, and if it is up to him, we won't talk at all. I have prayed over and over that we can work through this, and he will come back home. He hasn't. We go and sign the papers with our attorneys in a few days to finalize the divorce and each day is getting harder for me to get out of bed knowing that my marriage is over.

"The babies are doing just fine. Everything is right on schedule," Maci said, taking me away from my fucked-up thoughts.

As tears rolled down my face, Maci went to wash her hands and came over to me. She knows what is going on between Genesis and me. Other than her, Kai and Envii are all that I have right now. My sister is going through her own issues with E, so I try not to bother her unless I have to. When she is going through something, she makes the people that she deals with in the streets go through hell. That makes her feel better about everything. As I cry on Maci's shoulder, it just hit me like a ton of bricks that things are back to like they were before I met Genesis. I'm all alone again.

Somebody knocked on the door, and Maci told them to come in. I was surprised that it is Genesis. I never even bother telling him about my appointments. He asks me are we good, and I say yes, and that is the most we talk about the twins. I still can't believe that I am pregnant. It is something that I never thought would happen, but here it is.

Maci jumped up, so she can show Genesis the babies, and I just got even more uncomfortable with him being here. Genesis was always so loving and attentive to me, but now he is as cold as the mountains in December. I'm moving out of the house. I haven't told him yet, but I'm not staying in that big ass house by myself with two kids. I know he is going to be mad, but he'll get over it. He has no choice. He doesn't want me anymore.

I looked at Genesis as he watched the monitor looking at our kids, and he is smiling. That is something that I haven't seen in months. It caused me to start crying again. Genesis grabbed me and held me tight, but that just made me cry even harder.

* * *

"Envii, you have to get up," I said, opening the blinds in her bedroom.

Emanii has been at my house for a week, and Envii hasn't been answering any of her phones. I knew that this was going to be something that she didn't deal with well, but she can't stay in this room forever. Genesis and I are still in the same place we were before the ultrasound. I decided as we walked out of Dr. Maci's office that I have to just let him go if this is what he wants. I have to be stronger now than I ever have because in a few months before I know it I will have two kids depending on me. My sister has always been my rock, the person that I can always depend on to lean on, but since she gave E the divorce papers, she has been a mess.

"Envii, get the hell up!" I screamed, losing my patience.

Envii came from under the covers and leaned her back on the headboard. I told her to come downstairs so that she could eat. I came over to cook and get her out of this house. Emanii will be out of school in a few hours, and she wants to come home. My mom has been calling, but I haven't answered. I'm not telling Envii because right now beause she would be over there making good on her promise.

When Envii spit on Leonard at the funeral, we got escorted out. My mother was there, but we didn't say anything to each other. I really don't know what to say at this point. I feel like after all that has been done there is really nothing that can happen to bring us together. Right now, my only focus is myself and my kids.

"Alright, I'm out the bed, you can go home now!" Envii spat as she came into the kitchen.

Envii looks a mess. Her hair is all over her head. She has on one of E's too big t-shirts, a pair of E's boxers, and she just is not her regular self. I would never have thought that she would end up like this. Today is going to change all of that because we are going to help each other get through our divorces.

"I'm not going home because I'm moving in," I finally said.

I decided on the way over that I need to be here. I know that Genesis is going to still be mad because I'm leaving the house, but me coming to live with Envii I shouldn't have to argue for too long about it. I can tell by Envii's face that she doesn't want me living with her. She isn't going to tell me no, so I'm having a moving company move my stuff in a few days. The doorbell rang, so I got up to go and open the door.

"Mr. Jones, sent us here to pick up his property," a man said. I looked down the steps, and it's a moving company.

"Give me one minute," I said, closing the door behind me.

I already have a feeling this is not going to go well. She is already still mad. Why the fuck did I have to come over here today? I just hope that she doesn't try to do anything to the movers.

"Envii, the movers are here to get E's stuff," I said while standing in the doorway.

"That box behind you is everything that I didn't give to the Goodwill. Let them come get it," Envii said and proceeded to eat.

I looked behind me at the box and picked it up. There can't be really anything in this box. It has to be damn near empty. I handed it to the mover and told him that was everything. He is looking at me just as confused as I am that it is only this one box. I'm going to try to get Envii to go with me to see a therapist. I think she needs one now more than ever.

"I'll be right back," Envii said, pushing past me with a gun in each hand.

A YEAR LATER...

KAI

As Envii walked down the aisle, my hands started to sweat more. Katrina decided a week ago that if Envii was going to be in the wedding, then she wasn't going to be. Cariya is here though and is my maid of honor. Goddess is one of my bridesmaids too. Everything is perfect just like I wanted it to be. I know that I got on K's nerves while getting everything together, but everything that I wanted, he made happen.

Hope and Ta' Shell are the flower girls, and it is now our turn to walk down the aisle. K rented out a beautiful mansion in Beverly Hills, California for us to get married in. Well, up until yesterday I thought was rented until I saw the paperwork that said he bought it. As I get closer to K, I can see the tears in his eyes, which caused me to cry. I have been telling myself all morning that I wasn't going to cry today, but I guess I was wrong. As Jodeci "Love You For Life" plays in the background, I began to cry even harder.

As the preacher began to talk, I'm not listening to anything he was saying. I just want this to be over so that we can spend the rest of our lives together.

"Does anyone object to this union between Kai and Kamal? Speak now or forever hold your peace," the preacher said.

Hope started pulling on my dress wanting to be picked up. Kamal is looking at me like I better not pick her up, now she is screaming at the top of her lungs Gotti picked her up because she hasn't been feeling Mina since the baby. As Kamal and I kissed and sealed the deal, I know that this is going to last forever, and he is going to be the person that I am with until I take my last breath.

Kamal and I jumped the broom and made our way down the aisle with our wedding party behind us. K wanted to leave right after the wedding to go on our honeymoon. I talked him into having a reception, and we are leaving to go to Tulum, Mexico first thing in the morning. I looked back and saw that Mina and Ace are talking and laughing. I know that Mina has been seeing Ace, but I'm not getting in that. They both need to talk to K on their own. K and I got into a black Maybach to make our way to the reception.

We are going back to Denver for the reception, which is why I said that we should have just gotten married there. K insisted that he didn't want to get married there but wanted the reception to be there. We made our way to the airport and to the runway where the jets are waiting for us.

* * *

"You done crying, crybaby?" K asked, laughing.

"Shut up, nigga. You were crying too," I said as I fell into his arms.

K's phone started ringing, but he didn't answer. Cariya took my phone while I was getting my makeup done. Just like I expected none of my family came to my wedding except my Aunt Audrey. I would think that somebody would at least show up today, but they didn't. I have been in contact with Fat Stevie, but considering mine and K's history with him, we are taking it real slow with getting to know each other more. I confirmed with my mother that it was true that he was my father, and she hasn't talked to me since. As of right now, I'm letting that entire situation go and moving on with my life. The people that matter are here, and I know that they will always be.

As K and I got out of the car and made our way down the black carpet that is rolled out, K wrapped his arms around me and started kissing me as we made our way into the building. This past year has been a year that I will never forget. I finally have everything that I ever wanted and needed.

As we walked into the building, everything is like I requested. Envii had come up here earlier to cuss everybody out, so I am sure that is how it got done because this morning everything was not how it was supposed to be. As K and I walked through the room, I see Goddess and Gotti are so happy. I know that they have been through some shit, but I am happy that they worked things out for the boys. Envii and E are back together too. They took some time apart and decided to work things out.

"I'm about to go and hit a blunt I'll be right back," K said.

I made my way to change out of this dress. It was pretty, and I'm sure the pictures are beautiful, but it needs to come off now. I changed into the fitted black dress and heels that I had picked out to wear for tonight.

As I came out of the room from changing, Gotti asked me did I know where K was at. I told him outside, and he walked away. Once I got out to the main room, E is asking me where K is at too. I used Envii's phone to call K since Cariya has mine, and he didn't answer. I hung up and called back, and a nigga answered the phone.

"I hope you had a good time at yo wedding because you'll never see this nigga again!" the nigga spat and hung up.

I made my way outside to find E and Gotti with Envii on my heels. Out of all of the days for some shit to happen today. This is supposed to be one of the happiest days of my life. I found E and Gotti in the parking lot passing a blunt back and forth.

"Somebody's got K," I said as soon as I got up on them.

"Okay, we'll be right back," Gotti said.

"No, you won't. I'm going with y'all. It's that muthafucka Tyreek," I said.

I had been telling K that I didn't trust Tyreek. I don't want to hear all that brother shit. At first, I kept saying that I didn't trust Truth, but he hasn't done any shady shit, unlike Tyreek. After I heard Krack say that he wasn't happy about the position that Lady H put K in, I knew that he was still mad. That isn't some shit that you just get over.

"Envii, just stay here and make sure everything is good here," E said.

I don't give a fuck what neither one of them say I'm not staying here. I jumped in Gotti's car before he or E got in. I'm going with them to get K. Gotti's phone started ringing, and he answered, and Krack's voice came through the speakers.

"Where is K?" Krack asked.

"We don't know. We are trying to find him," I said as Gotti and E looked back at me all crazy.

"Has he been talking to Tyreek?" Krack asked.

"No, not since that shit that happened at Alice's funeral," I said before Gotti could answer.

Krack gave all the addresses where Tyreek may be at. Gotti stepped on the gas and made his way in the direction of the first location. What I don't understand is that regardless of what Tyreek does, his mom will never give him what she gave K. From my understanding he doesn't know how to handle the position, and that is why he didn't get it. I held on to my stomach as Gotti whipped in and out of traffic. I just pray that Kamal is okay for me and the baby's sake. I found out that I was pregnant earlier this week. I haven't even told K yet, and now this is happening.

"Kai, sit right and don't move!" Gotti spat.

Gotti and E jumped out of the car and made their way into the building. I am not going to be able to do this for much longer. Envii should have come with us. The longer I sit here, the more my mind starts to wonder. These minutes are starting to feel like hours.

Kurupt

As I sit in the back of this fucking truck in front of Union Station, I think I see Gotti getting out of his car. That nigga Tyreek is outside of the truck talking to somebody. I would never have imagined on my wedding day something like this would happen. As soon as I stepped outside to the back and lit my blunt, some six niggas walked up on me. Kai made me promise that I wouldn't bring a gun, and that is exactly why the fuck I'm sitting here right now.

I looked out the window, and the next thing I know bullets are flying through the fucking truck and the nigga in the front seat was hit in the head. As the door swung open, Gotti is attempting to get the lock busted that is on the chain as bullets are buzzing past our heads.

"Nigga, just bust the lock on my ankles so that I can get the fuck out this truck before we are both dead!" I screamed.

Gotti got the lock busted, and I got out the truck, and he finally got the lock on the chain that was tied around my back busted and handed me a gun. As I got out of the truck, I saw E is busting at the four niggas that are still standing. Gotti and E hit two of the niggas, and I'm trying to get Tyreek. I haven't seen or talked to this nigga since that shit happened at Alice's funeral. So, why now start this shit.

"You started this shit by taking my spot. I should have killed Krack too. He could go to be with yo momma!" Tyreek screamed out ducking behind a taxi cab.

"Bitch, if it were yo spot then you would have gotten it. Nigga, you should have stuck to business, but you couldn't do that I see!" I spat while Gotti is still shooting the fuck out of the cab.

"I should have just killed Giordan and Gionni since that bitch couldn't play her part either," Tyreek said.

Gotti heard that, and I know he is about to lose his mind about Gionni. As Tyreek went to come up to say some more shit, I took his head off and whatever he was about to say is dead with him It doesn't even matter. That means that all this time while we are all thinking that Giordan was trying to kill us because of some revenge shit with Gotti, it was this nigga sending me on dummy missions to kill his people.

I jumped in the back of Gotti's car, and Kai is in the back seat with head in her lap crying her eyes out. "Why the fuck is she here?" I asked as E and Gotti got in the car. I touched Kai's back, and she jumped up and wrapped her arms around my neck, squeezing it and still crying.

"I'm so happy that you're okay," Kai said in between crying.

"I'm good, stop crying," I said, hugging her.

"You want me to take you to the house?" Gotti asked.

"Naw, back to the party," I said, and Kai looked at me confused. She wanted this party so bad, so we are going back.

We pulled up to the reception venue, and we made our way through the back so that I can change my clothes. Gotti handed me a blunt before he disappeared down the hall to the main room. Kai made her way into the room set up for her so that she can get herself together. I can hear Mina's loud ass mouth screaming my name. As I jumped in the shower, the thought of not making it back here was never an option. I knew that somehow some way I was going to make it out of there.

As I got out the shower and threw on my clothes and made my way out the room, Kai was coming out of her room, and we made our way back into the party. Kai and I made our way over to the matching king and queen chairs that are sitting across the room. Once we sat down, Kai grabbed my hand and placed it on her stomach.

"For real?" I asked.

"Yea, I found out a few days ago," Kai said as I kissed her.

I would be lying if I said I knew that Kai and I would end up here. The shit that we went through was set up to break us and keep us from being together. We made it through all that shit, and it just made us stronger than we ever were. I know that this is going to last forever no matter what happens. The fact that Yellow accepted that an East Side Gangsta Chose her changed both of our lives forever.